I Am America

THE MINERS' LAMENT

A Story of Latina Activists in the
Empire Zinc Mine Strike

Book design by Jake Slavik
Illustrations by Eric Freeberg
Corrido translation by Santiago Pérez Muñoz

Photographs ©: John Fowler, 155 (top); Independent Production Company/Intl Union of Mine, Mill &a/Ronald Grant Archive/Alamy, 155 (bottom)

Published in the United States by Jolly Fish Press, an imprint of North Star Editions, Inc.

First Edition
First Printing, 2021

Library of Congress Cataloging-in-Publication Data (pending)
978-1-63163-535-9 (paperback)
978-1-63163-534-2 (hardcover)

Jolly Fish Press
North Star Editions, Inc.
2297 Waters Drive
Mendota Heights, MN 55120
www.jollyfishpress.com

Printed in the United States of America

I Am America

THE MINERS' LAMENT

A Story of Latina Activists in the Empire Zinc Mine Strike

By Judy Dodge Cummings

Illustrated by Eric Freeberg

Consultant: Zakery R. Muñoz, Syracuse University

JOLLY
FiSH
PRESS

Mendota Heights, Minnesota

A Note on Corridos

Corridos are traditional Mexican ballads. These songs tell stories, often about historical events in which the heroes fight injustice. The corrido as a musical form was developed in the 1800s and sung throughout Mexico. However, over time the corrido became known as "la música de la frontera"—the music of the border—because it was especially popular along both sides of the United States–Mexico border.

The corrido that appears in this story is in Spanish, but readers can find an English version in the back of the book on page 156.

Chapter 1

The church bell tolled four times. Ana Maria felt the vibrations deep in the hollow space where her heart used to be. She plucked at the strings of the vihuela cradled in her arms. If she could make music again, maybe she would not miss Mamá so much.

A gust of desert wind whooshed through the sagebrush and prodded her. The sun baked her black hair. A fly buzzed around her head. Ana Maria strummed a few chords on the vihuela and waited for words to come. Any words.

Then the fly landed on Ana Maria's chin. She swatted it and cried out, "What if I never write another song?"

No one answered, because the dead cannot speak. Ana Maria sat alone on the hill beside the wooden cross that marked Mamá's grave in the cemetery. Below her sprawled the small town of Alba, New Mexico. *Alba* means dawn, a time when the world is bright with possibility. But the town was the color of horse dung. The hills were brown. The brick church was brown. The shacks on the Mexican American side of town were brown. Except for one spot of color.

Ana Maria's eyes landed on the house Papá had built on land they rented from the Empire Zinc Company. The Garcia house was small. Two bedrooms, a tiny living room, an even tinier kitchen, a screened-in porch on the back of the house, and an outhouse in the backyard. The wooden fence that enclosed the yard was broken in a few spots, and the house's pine-plank siding was rough and weather-beaten. But the walls stood firm and straight.

The Garcias' front door was bright red, Mamá's favorite color. Every spring, she'd slapped on a new coat of paint so the door shone. Today was May 27, 1951. Spring was practically over. Who would paint the door this year?

Ana Maria's gaze skipped over the railroad tracks to the other side of town. The Empire Zinc Company had built decent houses for its Anglo workers. Each house had three bedrooms, a large living room, and a kitchen with a gas stove. Best of all, the Anglo houses had indoor plumbing. Resentment burned in Ana Maria's chest. If the company had put running water in the Mexican American homes, Mamá would still be alive.

In the Anglo neighborhood, James Wagner's house stood out. It was bigger than the rest and painted the color of honey. A neat fence ran around an emerald lawn. The house looked just as lovely inside as it did outside. James's father was a supervisor at the Empire Zinc Mine, and Mamá had been Mrs. Wagner's housekeeper for years. Ana Maria had spent countless hours in that house when she and James had still been friends.

About fifty yards up the road from the Wagner house was the arch that marked the entrance to Empire Zinc Company property. James must be able to see Papá and the other strikers from his living room window. Every day, these men marched on the picket line for higher pay and safer working conditions. For how many months had James been watching that scene? Ana Maria counted back. Union Local 890 went on strike on October 17, 1950, one week after Mamá had died.

Thick, unshed tears blocked Ana Maria's throat. She reached out one hand and traced the engraving on the cross.

TERESA ANA CARRANZA GARCIA

NOSOTROS TE AMAMOS SIEMPRE

1919–1950

The wood was warm from the sun, but lifeless. Ana Maria strummed the vihuela again. She felt closest to Mamá when she was playing the instrument that Mamá had given her.

Ana Maria had wanted to perform Mexican ballads since she was five years old. She and her parents had been visiting Mamá's parents in Ciudad Juárez, Mexico. Abuelo and his band were onstage, Grandpa singing and playing the guitarrón. Ana Maria was nestled on Papá's lap, her legs moving in time to the beat.

When the song ended, Ana Maria slid off Papá's lap and shouted, "When I grow up, I'm going to be a corridista like Abuelo!"

Everyone laughed. She hid her face in Papá's chest. "Why are they laughing at me?" she asked.

"They laugh because you are so little and have such big dreams," Mamá said.

"And they laugh," Papá added, "because you are a girl, and only boys can grow up to be corridistos."

Later that night, Ana Maria asked Abuelo if it was true that only boys could sing corridos.

"Ah, niña," Abuelo said, "the stage is no place for a woman. You'll marry and have babies and take care of your husband."

"But what will I do with my stories?" she asked.

"What stories?"

"All the stories in my head?"

Abuelo's old brow wrinkled. "Write them down."

"But they want to be sung."

"Sing me one," he commanded.

Her childish voice filled the room:

I'm going to sing a song,
About my gatito Ramón
His fur is jet black, and he is very fat
Because he hunts the ratón.

Abuelo clapped, and his deep laugh filled Ana Maria with a warm glow. But then he told her that corridos were not just made-up stories. They were history. They were songs about the struggles of the Mexican people and Mexican heroes who fought for justice. Someday, Abuelo said, she would have a brother. If she wrote corridos about important things, her brother would sing these songs onstage.

Ana Maria had thought about this. She wanted to perform corridos, not just compose them. Still, she wrote her songs down. Over the years, she filled a dozen notebooks with songs for a little brother who never came.

But Mamá had encouraged Ana Maria to do more than just write songs. Mamá gave Ana Maria the vihuela and told her that if being a corridista was her dream, she should never give it up. Since then, Ana Maria had been writing songs and playing them on her vihuela for anyone who would listen. But since Mamá's death, music had abandoned her.

Just then, a flash of yellow, blue, and black caught Ana Maria's eye. She looked up to see a swallowtail butterfly flit around Mamá's cross. The insect settled beside the epitaph. *Nosotros te amamos siempre.* We will always love you.

The words entered Ana Maria's mind so suddenly that she gasped. Grabbing her notebook and pencil, she began to write.

Amigos, vengan a escuchar mi historia de aflicción.
Ante ustedes he sido enviado
Para compartir esta historia sobre personas sencillas.
Aquí está su lamento.

Ana Maria strummed the vihuela, testing a tune. The music and lyrics fit together seamlessly. She inhaled deeply, and the tears that had been clogging her throat dissolved. The swallowtail rose from the cross, fluttered in the air, and flew away.

Ana Maria rose with a sense of purpose. She would write a corrido in honor of Mamá. For the moment at least, the sadness she had been carrying for months felt a little lighter.

Chapter 2

When Ana Maria arrived home, a blue truck was parked in front. Papá emerged from the house, carrying one end of the record console, the wooden cabinet that held Mamá's record player and albums. Their neighbor Javier Talamante held the other end.

"Papá," called Ana Maria, "where are you taking Mamá's console?" Mamá had talked Papá into buying it on credit last summer.

"We are behind on our payments," Papá said. He and Señor Talamante heaved the cabinet into the back of the truck. "Javier is driving me to Silver City so I can return it before the store sends someone out to repossess it." Papá climbed into the truck bed and tied the console in place.

"But Mamá's music," Ana Maria began.

"She isn't here to listen to music anymore." Papá did not look at her. "And I can't afford the payments. If the strike doesn't end soon, I'll have to sell your mother's vihuela next."

Ana Maria jerked back. "Mamá gave it to me. I can't write corridos without my vihuela."

Papá jumped down from the truck. "Listen, Ana Maria. The union helps us with utility bills and gives us groceries once a month, but it's not enough. Your corridos won't pay rent to Empire Zinc. We need dinero, not music. Besides, I've told you a hundred times. Only men can be corridistos."

Ana Maria frowned. Papá had always listened to her music, but he'd never believed in her the way Mamá had.

Señor Talamante rested one hand on Ana Maria's shoulder. "Don't worry about the record player, mija. Your madre is listening to the music of angels now."

Tears pricked Ana Maria's eyes. She looked down at her dust-covered chanclas.

"Maybe you can come over later and play with Gabriela," Señor Talamante said.

"Gracias." Gabriela was his daughter and Ana Maria's best friend. She lived two houses away.

"Vamos, Javier," Papá said. "I'll be back in an hour, Ana Maria."

She nodded but kept her head down. Then Papá's finger was under her chin, gently lifting her head up.

"I know you are sad, mija." The bite was gone from Papá's voice. His eyes were weary. "But it is better to return the record player, no? We don't need this painful memory sitting in the corner."

"But where should we put Mamá's ofrenda?" Ana Maria asked. She had displayed a collection of photographs, flowers, and candles in Mamá's memory on top of the cabinet.

A flash of pain filled Papá's eyes. He blinked and it disappeared. "I took the altar down."

Ana Maria gasped.

"I couldn't—" Papá turned away, the muscles of his jaw working hard. "Looking at those photographs every day—" He turned to Ana Maria again. His expression told her not to push the issue. "I just had to take it down."

You had no right! I built that shrine for Mamá. The words battered the insides of her mouth, trying to escape. But

Papá insisted on obedience and respect from his daughter, and Ana Maria always complied. She pressed her lips together to trap the angry words.

After Papá left, Ana Maria went into the house. She slipped the vihuela case off her back and propped it in the corner of the living room. Then she entered the tiny kitchen and groaned. Mamá had cooked breakfast, lunch, and dinner every day, year after year. Now Papá expected Ana Maria to do the same. But she hated cooking.

She dumped one cup of rice into a saucepan. Luckily, Papá had filled the water barrel this morning from the pump in the yard. She scooped two cups of water from the barrel and added that to the pan. She filled the stove's firebox with kindling, struck a match, and held it to the wood.

How many times had she watched Mamá perform this very task? As the flame licked a piece of wood, a memory flared in Ana Maria's mind.

Seven-year-old Ana Maria was begging Mamá to teach her how to play the vihuela. "You never play it, Mamá. It's covered in dust."

"I need to get this pollo in the pot," Mamá said, standing at the kitchen counter.

"Papá can cook supper."

Mamá laughed. "Did you hear that, Martín?"

Papá, stretched out on the sofa and drinking beer, chuckled. "I worked all day in the mine, digging out zinc."

Ana Maria studied her father. "Then you can teach me how to play the vihuela."

Papá snorted. "I don't know how to play it."

She frowned. "Then you must cook the pollo so Mamá can teach me."

"I don't know how to cook pollo either," Papá said.

Ana Maria plopped down on the sofa. "But if I don't learn to play the vihuela, how can I be a corridista?"

He leaned over and gently tugged her hair. "I've already told you, mi querida. Boys sing corridos, not girls."

"I *can*, Papá," she insisted. "Listen to what Abuelo taught me." She slid off the sofa, clasped her hands behind her back, and sang an old ballad about the Mexican Revolution. Her voice soared, high and clear. Mamá clapped, but Papá burst out laughing.

"Martín," Mamá scolded. "Don't laugh. You sound lovely, Ana Maria."

Papá ran one hand over his mouth as though trying to wipe away his grin. "Your singing is lovely, mija, but the vihuela will be saved for your brother."

"I don't have a brother," Ana Maria shot back. A shadow of pain crossed Mamá's face. Ana Maria wished she had kept her mouth shut. In the last three years, Mamá had had three miscarriages.

"Someday you will," Papá said. "Meanwhile, the vihuela must be kept safe for a boy to carry on the family tradition."

"But Abuelo gave the vihuela to Mamá, and she's a girl."

"Enough," Papá said. He walked into the kitchen and lifted the lid of a pot on the stove. "How much longer, Teresa? I'm hungry."

Suddenly, Ana Maria felt a flame lick her finger. The memory vanished. She tossed the match into the firebox.

In minutes, the rice was simmering and Ana Maria was sweltering. Once again, she thought of James Wagner's house and its gas stove, where with a flick of the wrist, the flame turned on or off.

Fanning herself with one hand, Ana Maria went into the living room. The corner where the record player had stood with Mamá's ofrenda was now bare. All that remained of the colorful papel picado Ana Maria had hung was a torn scrap of green tissue paper dangling halfway up the wall. Gone, too, were the candles she'd lit every evening and the framed photographs of Mamá.

The living room looked as sad as Ana Maria felt. The green-flowered sofa slouched along one wall. A wad of paper shoved under the short leg of the table kept it from wobbling. A painting of Benito Juárez hung over the sofa. He was the founding father of Mexico whom Papá most admired. Ana Maria thought Juárez's eyes looked sad—as if the sight of how the Garcias lived was proof that the reforms he'd fought for almost one hundred years earlier had not solved the problems of poor Mexican Americans.

The mail lay on the table. One opened envelope caught her eye. She removed the letter and read it.

To Our Employees,

The leadership of Union Local 890 is leading you astray. Did you know that Scott Bradley, the representative sent by the International Union of Mine, Mill, and Smelters, is a communist? Communism is a threat to the American way of life. Do you really want to follow Bradley's advice?

You have suffered enough. Empire Zinc wants to bring you back to work. But the communist leadership of your union is preventing that.

Ana Maria frowned. Communism? She did not know what that word meant. Papá said Scott Bradley was the best Anglo he had ever met. But this letter made him sound dangerous.

A notebook lay open on the table. Papá's angry reply to the company practically leaped off the paper. A spider of anxiety scurried up Ana Maria's spine. The strike was in its eighth month. If the rest of the union felt like Papá, the battle was far from over. She looked at her vihuela case leaning against the wall. Suddenly, the instrument looked too exposed, too vulnerable. She carried it to her bedroom.

The small room was neat and spare. A pine dresser with a mirror stood along one wall. Under the room's lone window was an iron-framed bed covered in a bright quilt.

Papá's words echoed through her mind. *If the strike doesn't end soon, I'll have to sell your mother's vihuela next.* She shoved the instrument under her bed.

Ana Maria sat on the stool in front of the dresser. Tucked in the mirror's frame was her favorite photograph of her mother. Mamá and Abuelo stood side by side. He was playing the guitarrón and she was playing the vihuela. Mamá was young, fourteen or fifteen. Her dark hair was pulled back in braids and her eyes glittered. Two huge dimples punctuated her smile.

Ana Maria swallowed hard. If Papá ordered her to give him the vihuela to sell, she would have to turn it over. But the very thought made her heart ache. The vihuela was her heritage, passed down from Abuelo to Mamá and now to her. Without the vihuela, she could not communicate the history of her life. Giving up her vihuela would be like giving up her voice.

But Ana Maria knew she could not defy Papá by refusing to give him the instrument. Instead, she would help him. She would find a way to raise money to pay the bills.

Chapter 3

Ana Maria's first chance to earn money came one week later on the last day of school. The top ten spellers from fourth and fifth grade were competing in the school spelling bee. Ana Maria and nine other students sat onstage in front of a packed gymnasium. Some parents were present, but not Papá. He was on the picket line.

"I hope I go out in the first round," said Larry Jensen, the fifth grader sitting to Ana Maria's left. "I'm so nervous, I might puke."

James reached over Larry and swatted Ana Maria on the knee. "My mom's trying to catch your attention." He nodded toward the audience.

Mrs. Wagner looked like she had been cut out of a magazine advertisement. Her blonde hair was perfectly styled, and her pink lipstick matched her pink sweater. She was waving wildly. "Good luck," she mouthed.

Ana Maria smiled awkwardly and waved back. She had not seen Mrs. Wagner for months. With Mamá gone, there was no reason to go to the Wagner house anymore. But clearly Mrs. Wagner thought she and James were still friends.

Ana Maria glanced at James. He was now staring straight ahead, ignoring her.

After Ana Maria was born, Mamá had brought her along when she worked at the Wagner house. Ana Maria and James had shared the same toys and napped together in the same playpen. They'd been in the same classroom every day from kindergarten through fifth grade. Though Mexican Americans and Anglos were segregated throughout New Mexico, Alba was too small a town to afford separate schools. After school, Ana Maria and James had walked to the Wagner house together and finished their homework at the kitchen table while Mamá prepared the Wagners' dinner.

Then Mamá had died and everything had changed.

Ana Maria remembered James offering her condolences in school the day after the funeral. The words had galloped out of her—accusing his father, a supervisor for Empire Zinc, of having killed Mamá. James had gotten angry, of course. Ana Maria had wanted to explain. The thoughts were so clear in her mind: If Empire Zinc had given the Mexican American workers indoor plumbing and gas stoves, Mamá wouldn't have needed to chop wood to heat water for cooking and washing. If she hadn't need-ed to chop wood, she wouldn't have accidentally cut her-self with the ax. The wound wouldn't have gotten infected. Mamá wouldn't have died.

But when Ana Maria tried to explain, her agitated thoughts had spilled in a tumble of Spanish, a language James did not understand. Her teacher had scolded her for not speaking English, and James had walked away from their friendship.

Ana Maria shook her head to dispel the memory. She smoothed her dress over her legs. Mrs. Wagner had wished her good luck in the spelling bee. But skills were better than luck, and Ana Maria was a skilled speller.

Papá had lived in El Paso for several years as a child, so he grew up bilingual. Mamá, on the other hand, had not spoken a word of English when she'd married Papá and migrated to Alba. Determined to succeed in America, Mamá had bought a Spanish-English dictionary and studied it religiously. When Ana Maria was old enough, she and Mamá had held vocabulary contests. Ana Maria believed she could out-spell everyone onstage.

Still, she would take any good luck Mrs. Wagner wanted to send her. The winner of the spelling bee would go on to the regional competition in Silver City. The prize for that contest was five dollars! That money might save her vihuela.

The spelling bee began, and the competition narrowed. Before long, only three spellers remained: James Wagner, Peter Long, and Ana Maria. For several rounds, all three of them spelled every word correctly. Then James got the word *sanitation*. He groaned, and everyone laughed. He spelled the word with three *a*'s instead of two.

Ana Maria bit back a smile. She knew how to spell this word. Last fall, Mamá had grown so tired of having to haul and heat water that she'd written a letter to the superintendent of the Empire Zinc Company to complain about the lack of saneamiento on the Mexican side of town. Although Mamá had become a competent English speaker, she could not write the language well. So, she'd written the letter in Spanish and asked Ana Maria to translate it. *Sanitation* had been one of the words Ana Maria had looked up.

"Ana Maria," said Mr. Larson, the librarian. "Please spell *sanitation*."

Ana Maria stood up, feeling confident.

"Sanitation. S-a-n-i- . . ." Suddenly, the audience receded. Images flashed in Ana Maria's mind. The deep gouge in Mamá's foot. Papá trying to treat the wound himself, since they could not afford a doctor. Mamá burning with fever as the wound grew infected. Mamá in a hospital bed in Silver City, receiving treatment too late. Mamá dying.

Ana Maria shook her head to chase away the horrible images. But her ability to spell *sanitation* vanished. The audience stared as she frantically searched her brain. Students began to whisper. Heat burned her cheeks.

Unable to bear the spotlight a moment longer, Ana Maria began again. "Sanitation. S-a-n-e-a-m-i-e-n-t-o." She dropped back into her seat.

Peter snickered.

Mr. Larson frowned. "Well, that is the correct *Spanish* spelling of the word." He looked to the principal.

Mr. Swallow shook his head. "Ana Maria knows perfectly well that we only speak English in school. That's incorrect."

Mr. Larson gave Ana Maria an apologetic smile. Then he turned to Peter. "Mr. Long, please spell *sanitation*."

Peter rattled off the correct spelling. Easy enough, since James had already given him every correct letter but one.

"To win the contest, Peter," Mr. Larson said, "you must first spell one more word correctly. That word is *independence*."

The fifth graders in the audience laughed. They had just finished learning about the American Revolution. *Independence* had been one of their spelling words. A cocky smile twisted Peter's mouth. He gave the correct spelling.

Everyone clapped as Peter stepped forward to claim his winning certificate. Ana Maria rose slowly and followed James down the stage steps, still shaken by the image of Mamá's sickly face.

Mrs. Wagner hurried over. She gave her son a quick hug and smiled at Ana Maria. "Second and third place, you two. Good job."

Ana Maria gave a weak smile.

Mrs. Wagner reached into her purse and pulled out a handful of root beer candies. "You're both champions in my book. Here are your runner-up prizes."

She dropped several candies into their hands. James immediately unwrapped one and popped it into his mouth.

"Hmm, root beer barrels," he said. "Aren't these great, Ana Maria?" He was mocking her. He knew she hated the taste of root beer.

Ana Maria slipped the candies into her pocket and thanked Mrs. Wagner. Then she took her place in the line of students heading back to their classrooms. A few students down, James stood laughing at something Larry said.

A familiar loneliness draped its arm around Ana Maria's shoulders. She seemed to be losing everything these days. Mamá. James's friendship. Now she might lose her vihuela too. She hurt so much inside, and no one understood. Whenever she tried to explain her feelings, the words came out wrong, just like the letters had in the spelling bee today. It was as if something had stolen part of her voice. She could speak, but no one could understand what she really meant.

An idea sprang into Ana Maria's mind. Reaching into the pocket of her dress, she retrieved the little notebook and pencil she always carried. She began to write. She wanted to record these lyrics to Mamá's corrido before she forgot them.

Siendo el diez de octubre,
Frescura caía al anochecer,
Cuando la mujer llamada Teresa
Olía el almizcle corromper.

Mientras cortaba leña
Ella la noche observó.
Y unos ojos rojos brillantes, mandíbulas dentadas—
Ella lo reconoció.

Cucuy lanzó un llamado
Con apetito indómito,
Hambriento por la hija de Teresa
Quién fuera permanecía durmiendo.

SILVER CITY DAILY

June 9, 1951

SHERIFF VOWS TO KEEP THE PEACE ON THE PICKET LINE

Empire Zinc Company announced the mine will reopen on June 11 with new employees. Grant County sheriff Thomas Coleman has deputized local men to keep the peace. Coleman insists he will clamp down on all violence, whether it comes from strikebreakers trying to cross the picket line or striking miners trying to stop them.

Chapter 4

After reading the paper over Papá's shoulder, Ana Maria sat down across from him. "Are you worried, Papá?"

He took a sip of coffee and shrugged. "I voted for Coleman last year. I think he's a decent man."

"Can I come with you on Monday and watch with the women?" she asked. School had been out for a week.

Papá frowned. "A picket line is no place for a girl. I don't even think the Ladies Auxiliary should be there."

"Mamá was in the auxiliary."

"Yes, but that was when all they did was organize pot-lucks and play bingo."

Ana Maria felt a prick of irritation. "Gabriela will be there. Her papá wants her to witness la gente standing up for their rights."

Papá looked at her over the top of the newspaper. "Javier said that?"

She nodded.

He rubbed his chin. "Huh, let me think about it."

And so, Monday morning, Ana Maria found herself riding in the back of the Talamantes' truck beside Gabriela. The cool air carried the scent of sagebrush. Ana Maria watched as they turned onto Zinc Hill Road and crested a hill. At the bottom of the hill, Señor Talamante pulled off the road. Ana Maria sat up and looked around.

To the left of the road, the ground fell away into a deep gully. To the road's right was a small grassy hill. A wooden arch crossed the road about fifty feet ahead. About a half mile beyond the arch stood a mountain of dirt, gravel, and rubble. The road wound up the mountain to a tower that marked the opening of the zinc mine shaft.

A dozen men marched back and forth across the narrow road in front of the arch. More men sat at the foot of the hill, waiting for their turn on the picket line. About thirty members of the Ladies Auxiliary stood behind the miners. Their skirts flapped in the breeze like battle flags.

Sheriff Coleman and his deputies stood on the gully side of the road. The khaki-clad men wore cowboy hats

and holsters hung low on their hips. Sheriff Coleman was rail-thin and wore thick glasses. He looked more like an accountant than a cowboy.

Papá turned to Ana Maria. "You stay on that hill with the women."

Ana Maria and Gabriela ran up the hill and sat in the grass beside Señora Morano. The old widow's husband had been killed in a mine accident twenty years ago.

A red car that Ana Maria recognized drove up to the picket line. Mr. Wagner rolled down his window. Scott Bradley, the union rep, walked over to talk to him. Ana Maria recalled what the letter from the company had said about Mr. Bradley.

She whispered to Gabriela, "What's a communist?"

Gabriela frowned. "Somebody who doesn't eat meat?"

"That's a vegetarian."

"Oh, yeah. Um, I think a communist is someone who doesn't believe in God."

"That's an atheist."

Gabriela laughed. "I have no clue then."

"Brothers!" Mr. Bradley shouted. "Let Mr. Wagner through." The picketers parted, and James's father drove under the arch.

"Why does he get to cross the picket line?" Gabriela asked.

"Wagner is management," Señora Morano explained. "The bosses are allowed in."

Once past the arch, Mr. Wagner stopped the car. The back door opened and James, Larry, and Peter emerged. The boys settled down on the grass, leaning against the wooden beam of the arch on the gully side of the road.

Señora Morano clicked her tongue. "The white boys have come to watch the show."

Ana Maria caught James's eye, but he looked away.

"Uh-oh," the widow said. "Here come the scabs."

Two cars loaded with men drove slowly toward the picket line.

Ana Maria knew *scab* was another term for strikebreaker. These were men willing to cross the picket line to take the job of a striking worker. All the men in the cars were Anglos.

"I've received orders from the district attorney to clear the road," the sheriff called to the strikers. "Clear off, men, or you'll be arrested."

The miners looked to Mr. Bradley. The union rep was not budging. "We prepared for this, brothers," Mr. Bradley said. "You know what to do."

Ana Maria prayed that Papá would obey the sheriff. If he went to jail, she would be all alone. But Papá widened his stance and crossed his arms.

Sheriff Coleman unclipped a pair of handcuffs from his belt and walked up to Mr. Bradley. The union leader held out his hands. But as soon as the sheriff led him to a squad car, one of the men on the hill took Mr. Bradley's place on the picket line.

A deputy hauled away the next picketer. Another miner filled the gap. So it went. The place of each man arrested was filled by one of the men waiting on the hillside.

Ana Maria watched with growing anxiety as the deputies worked their way down the line to Papá. When a deputy took his arm, Papá did not struggle, nor did he cooperate. He stood as solid as an oak tree. Frustrated, the deputy twisted Papá's arm and forced him to bend.

Ana Maria leaped to her feet and charged down the hill. When she reached the deputy, the man stuck out his arm. Ana Maria barreled into it. The impact knocked her onto the grass.

As Papá was led away, he frowned at her. "I told you to stay on the hill. Vete a casa! Go home."

Ana Maria's lower lip began to wobble. Someone snickered. She turned to see Peter standing nearby, laughing. James and Larry still sat in front of the arch, both of them staring at her.

"What are you, Ana Maria?" Peter called. "A football player? I can't believe you tried to tackle a deputy."

She glared at him.

"Do you know what they do to communists like your dad?" Peter said. "They send them to Russia."

My dad isn't a communist! Ana Maria opened her mouth to yell but felt a sob bubble up her throat instead. She snapped her jaws together to hold it back.

James stood up and nudged Larry. "Let's go to my house and toss a ball around."

Without waiting to see if Peter would follow, James strode north along the shoulder of the road. As he walked past, he glanced at Ana Maria out of the corner of his eye. Her cheeks grew hot as she imagined how silly she must have looked as she bounced off that deputy's arm.

Later, Señor Talamante drove Ana Maria and Gabriela back to his house. He assured Ana Maria that her papá would be bailed out of jail soon—the union would pay the fee. So, she tried to stay busy, organizing Gabriela's rock collection, playing tic-tac-toe with Gabriela's brothers, and helping Gabriela's mother shell peas. But she kept looking at the clock. When would Papá come home?

Finally, at eight o'clock, Papá was dropped off at the Talamantes' house. He and Ana Maria walked home as the sun sank below the horizon. He was exhilarated.

"We stuck to Bradley's plan. No scabs got through the picket line. No zinc was mined today! If we get support from other unions, we're going to bring Empire Zinc to its knees!" He grinned at her.

She smiled back. His enthusiasm was infectious. "I hope so. I was frightened when you were arrested."

They had reached their house. As Papá opened the gate, his smile faded. "Why did you plow into that deputy today? I told you to stay on the hill."

"I got scared. When I saw that man twist your arm, I didn't think."

"That's the problem." Papá strode up the path and opened the front door. "You don't think. The picket line is no place for a young girl."

"But I want to do something to help."

He patted her on the head. "You can help by fixing me some supper. I'm starving."

Papá went to his room, but Ana Maria stayed in the entryway. *Dogs get patted on the head, not daughters.* The thought felt like a little seed of fire on her tongue that she wanted to spit at Papá. Instead, she went to the water barrel in the kitchen, filled the dipper, and drank deeply. The resentment burned as she swallowed it.

A little later, Papá delivered bad news through a mouthful of rice and beans. "I learned about a man in Silver City who buys musical instruments. If negotiations with the company don't improve in the next two weeks, we'll need cash."

Ana Maria said nothing. She just retreated to her bedroom, took her notebook from the dresser drawer, and climbed into bed. How could Papá sell the vihuela? It was *hers*. Mamá had given it to her on her eighth birthday. Though Papá had frowned, Mamá had pulled Ana Maria into a hug and whispered, "Your papá thinks you are too young. But your abuelo gave me this vihuela when I turned eight. You have music in your heart, querida. You are old enough. Never give up your dreams."

Now, Ana Maria wondered what dreams Mamá had never achieved, with her life stolen from her so young.

Teresa de pie se puso para defender
Al bebé que dentro de la casa permanecía.
Cucuy llegó a un acuerdo con ella—
Donde a cambio de un préstamo la vida de la niña le daría.

La mujer la dio siguiendo su voluntad;
Ella no tenía otra opción.
Por la vida de su hija se debía sacrificar
Ofreció la voz profunda de su corazón.

Aún cuando Teresa pudiera hablar,
Tenía prohibido revelar
Todos los pensamientos que habían dentro de su corazón
Que ocultos para siempre deberían estar.

Chapter 5

 $\mathcal{A}$ lthough the picket line had held, Empire Zinc was not giving up the fight. The next day, Papá told Ana Maria to prepare an early supper. Sheriff Coleman had delivered a court order to Ricardo Torrez, the union president. Everyone from the mining community was meeting at the union hall in Bayard that evening to vote on how to respond.

The union headquarters was a single-story beige structure. From the outside, it was about as bland as a building could be. Inside was a different story. There were colorful campaign posters for political candidates. Mexican woodcuts showed scenes of women kneading bread, farmers tilling fields, and revolutionaries swinging swords. Sign-up sheets were taped along one wall. Volunteers could sign up to walk the picket line, address envelopes, organize donations, or join committees. At the front of the room was a rectangular table with five chairs for the union leaders. An American flag was draped across the wall behind the chairs. Beside it hung a bright yellow banner with the words "An injury to one is an injury to all."

The miners sat on folding chairs in the middle of the hall, while women and children filled the benches along the walls. Ana Maria squeezed between Gabriela and Linda Bradley, the fourteen-year-old daughter of Scott Bradley.

A tall middle-aged man with a waistline the size of the equator rose from the front table and banged a gavel until the room quieted.

"If you don't know me," the big man said, "I'm Ricardo Torrez, the president of Local 890. These men"—he gestured to the men sitting on either side of him—"are the executive board. We've called this meeting because we have to make a choice."

Señor Torrez withdrew a piece of paper from his pocket. "Today, Sheriff Coleman dropped off this little gift from Judge John Sanders." He shook the paper. "Listen up."

Sixth Judicial District Court
Grant County, State of New Mexico

Members of Local 890 Mine-Mill Union are hereby RESTRAINED from physically obstructing, blocking, or otherwise preventing access to the entrance of the Empire Zinc Company from Zinc Hill Road.

The legal mumbo jumbo confused Ana Maria, but when he finished reading the document, Señor Torrez summed things up. "If we obey the injunction and stop picketing, scabs will move in and fill our jobs. Mining operations will begin, and we'll lose the strike."

"Then we must disobey the injunction!" Papá shouted.

Señor Torrez held up one hand. "If we defy the court, we'll be arrested. Then we'll lose the strike anyway because we'll all be in jail."

At the front table, Scott Bradley stood. "There you have it, brothers. Empire Zinc has us between a rock and a hard place. It's your choice. We are a democratic union, so tonight we'll vote on our next step."

Señor Torrez banged his gavel and opened the floor for discussion. The men tossed out ideas:

"Call a general strike!"

"That's crazy. We'd never get support from miners in other states."

"We have to obey the injunction. The union can't afford to bail out everyone, and I can't afford to sit in jail."

"You want to give up? After all this time and sacrifice?"

Ana Maria felt the air thicken with despair and frustration. The mood and the heat made it hard to breathe. Then Gabriela's mother, Juana Talamante, raised her hand. Señor Torrez called on her. Señora Talamante stood up, balancing her three-year-old son Carlos on her hip.

"Am I correct that the court order only prevents the miners from picketing?"

"That's right," said Señor Torrez.

Señora Talamante gestured to the women around the room. "We are not miners. The women can cover the picket line."

The hall was completely silent for a moment. Then Papá let out a bark of laughter.

"Don't laugh at me, Martín Garcia," Señora Talamante scolded. "I don't hear a better solution. Remember, if you lose this strike, your wives and children suffer too." She hoisted little Carlos into the air. "This is our fight as well."

Admiration swelled in Ana Maria's chest. She wished she had as much courage as Gabriela's mother.

Señor Torrez banged the gavel, and the debate on her proposal began. Soon, the room smelled like coffee and confrontation. The din of voices was accompanied by the screech of chairs and the whine of children.

"We'll be the laughingstock of the labor movement if women take over the picket line," one miner said.

"Better to be laughed at than to lose," another man shot back.

"The picket line is not a proper place for women," said Papá.

Señor Talamante raised one hand. "I think we should give the women a chance. They'd be like a secret weapon. The bosses will not expect skirts on the picket line."

Papá looked at his friend in surprise. "Really, Javier? You would risk your wife that way?"

Señor Talamante laughed and jerked his head toward his wife. "It was her idea in the first place."

Papá stood up. "Think about it. What will happen when the police start beating up our women? Are we going to just sit on the hillside and watch? No! We'll jump in to protect them, and then we'll be arrested. We're back to square one." He surveyed the room. "And have you even considered that if the women are on the line all day, who's going to take care of the children and do the cooking and the washing?"

Some of the women groaned and rolled their eyes.

Papá whacked Señor Talamante on the arm. "If Juana is on the picket line all day, you're going to have to change Carlito's diapers."

The miners burst into laughter.

Señora Talamante walked over and handed Carlos to her husband. "I'll have you know, Martín, that Carlos doesn't wear diapers anymore, and Javier isn't afraid of a little hard work."

The men laughed even harder.

Señor Torrez banged the gavel. "We must get serious. We need to decide on a strategy."

Señora Morano rose and walked to the front of the room. As the old woman surveyed the miners through hooded eyes, the laughter died away.

"Women have as much stake in this strike as men do." Her voice was soft but powerful. "We are the ones who have to feed our children on the meager wages the company pays. We are the ones who have to mourn our loved ones when their mangled corpses are pulled out from a mine that the company refuses to keep safe."

The words pierced Ana Maria's heart. A tidal wave of emotion rose inside her. She stood, and words tumbled out of her mouth. "And we are the ones who have to bury our mothers when they hurt themselves chopping wood because the company refuses to put plumbing in our houses!"

Everyone stared at her. Ana Maria dropped back onto the bench and looked at her knees. Doubt crept up her spine. For a long moment, the hall was quiet.

"The girl is right," Señora Morano said.

Surprised, Ana Maria looked up.

"Three years ago, the union asked for indoor plumbing," the old woman continued. "When the company refused, you just caved in." She threw out an accusatory hand at Señor Torrez and Mr. Bradley. Then she turned a fierce stare on Papá. "And Martín, you say if the police threaten women on the picket line, the men will jump in and protect us. The women don't need your protection on the line. What we need—what your wife needed—are better wages and indoor plumbing."

Papá's face turned deep red. Ana Maria knew this color did not mean he was embarrassed. It meant he was furious.

A bead of nervous sweat trickled between her shoulder blades. What would Papá say when they got home?

After much more debate, Señor Torrez declared it was time to vote. Because the issue concerned the women, enough men agreed that women should be permitted to vote on the question. Señor Torrez called for a show of hands. Should female relatives of the miners take the place of the strikers on the picket line? Papá voted no, as did several other men. But because the women were also allowed to take part, the yes vote carried the day. The women would walk the picket line.

After Señor Talamante dropped them off, Papá stalked into the house. Ana Maria barely caught the front door before it slammed in her face.

Papá sat down on the couch and began yelling. "Do you know how long we've been on strike, Ana Maria?"

"Yes." She sat down in the rocking chair.

"Do you?" Papá's tone made it clear that he did not believe her. "Do you really?"

"The strike started—"

Papá cut in. "Because we have been fighting for—"

"—one week after Mamá died."

"—important issues that you don't under—" He trailed off. His scowl shifted into an expression Ana Maria could not read.

"Mamá died on October 10," she continued, "and the strike started October 17."

Papá turned to stare out the window. His voice was low and rough. "What I'm trying to say is that you should not have brought your mother's death into the discussion."

His condemnation stung. "But Empire Zinc should give us hot water," Ana Maria said. "Mamá wrote to the company herself asking them to put plumbing in our house."

Papá snorted in disbelief. "She never did."

"Yes, she did. I translated the letter for her last fall."

Papá gripped his hair with both hands and tugged, as if trying to yank her words from his mind. "You humiliated me tonight by blurting out in the meeting. Just like the other day when you plowed into that deputy." He slammed one fist into the couch. "People must think I have no control over my own daughter."

"But, Papá—"

"I don't want to hear another word. Go to bed, Ana Maria."

Inside her room, Ana Maria paced. She did not understand Papá. Why wasn't he fighting for the thing that would have saved Mamá? Why was he upset that she had spoken up? Somewhere in the desert hills, a coyote howled. It was a haunting, lonely sound.

Ana Maria lit a candle and put it on the dresser. She looked at her flickering reflection in the mirror and saw both her parents reflected back. She had Mamá's jutting chin and full mouth. But her eyes tilted slightly upward like Papá's. *Cucuy appears in many guises when he comes to steal a voice. Sometimes even disguised as the people closest to us.*

Por supuesto su espíritu se desgarraría
Teresa tuvo que quebrar su maldición.
Así volvió hacia su amada
Pero algo peor encontró.

Mi amor, rogó, por favor escucha.
Cucuy ha silenciado mis sueños.
Pero cuando la miró a los ojos
Teresa solo pudo gritar.

Dentro del hombre que Teresa amaba
Moraba la bestia de ojos rojos.
Enfrentó al minero contra la esposa del minero;
Para hacer en su disputa festejos.

Chapter 6

The next day, Papá forbade Ana Maria from going anywhere. So, she mopped the floors, dusted the furniture, and did the laundry. Then she baked conchas, Papá's favorite sweet bread, and made enough frijoles de la olla to last for days. Once these chores were finished, she waited. Her body was tired, but her mind was restless. What was happening at the mine?

In the early evening, Ana Maria sat on the front step. A car pulled up in front of the house, and Papá climbed out. He strolled up the path and sat down beside her. His relaxed smile was so unlike the worried frown he had worn during breakfast.

"The line held today," Papá said, gazing into the hills.

"That's good."

"The sheriff left the women alone."

"Really?"

"There were lots of kids there today, even Gabriela. When Javier came to pick up Juana, he brought the kids along to watch for a while."

Envy pricked Ana Maria. The Talamantes were more relaxed than Papá when it came to what girls could and could not do.

Papá chuckled. "Carlito even marched beside his mamá for a while. He strutted like a little rooster."

His laughter chafed Ana Maria. Papá admired a three-year-old boy who marched, but he would not let his own eleven-year-old daughter watch from the sidelines?

"I'll get dinner." She started to rise.

"Wait, mija." Papá put a hand on her arm. "Lupe Bernal asked for you to babysit her daughter this Saturday."

Ana Maria sighed. She supposed babysitting was better than housekeeping. "What time?"

Papá had a thoughtful expression on his face. "She wants you all day. At the picket line."

Ana Maria drew back in surprise. "At the picket line?"

"Sí, she wants to march, but she is still nursing, so she needs her baby nearby."

Please, please, please, let me go. Ana Maria wanted to beg, but the tightness in her throat warned her to swallow her words instead. Speaking just got her into trouble.

Papá ran a finger across his upper lip. "I told her you could do it on one condition. You must stay far away from the picket line." His voice was stern.

"Sí, Papá." Her heart hammered with excitement.

Two days later, Ana Maria followed Lupe Bernal as the woman rolled a stroller into an open-sided hut the strikers had put up for shade. Señora Bernal's five-month-old baby, Angelina, was asleep in the stroller. Ana Maria sat down on a picnic table inside the hut.

"When she wakes up, bounce her on your knee," Señora Bernal said. "If she gets fussy, yell for me and I'll come feed her." She handed Ana Maria a diaper bag and headed off to join the scores of women who had come from Alba, Santa Rita, Hurley, and Bayard. The women took shifts on the picket line, at least a dozen blocking the road at a time.

When the managers began to arrive for the workday, Juana Talamante checked each car to make sure no scabs were inside before she let the bosses pass. Once again, Mr.

Wagner drove up with James in the car beside him. Ana Maria's stomach sank when she saw Peter in the back seat. Larry was not with them today. James and Peter sat near the mine arch to watch the action, less than twenty feet from where Ana Maria sat.

Chatter and laughter filled the air. A miner played the guitar and sang folk songs in a rich baritone. Señora Bernal linked arms with two other women, and they danced across the road instead of marching. Ana Maria itched to join them. If Mamá were alive, she would be dancing too.

A breeze drifted through the hut. Ana Maria gently rocked the stroller. She felt something stir deep inside, something that felt like hope. Although not on the picket line herself, Ana Maria knew she was helping someone else march. Playing this small part in the miners' fight felt good.

A green car approached the picket line with an Anglo man behind the wheel. Sheriff Coleman and the deputies all watched it. The vehicle moved slowly toward the marching women.

Thirty feet away. Then twenty. Fifteen.

Señora Talamante stood in the center of the road, her hands on her hips. "That car is full of scabs!" she yelled.

Señora Bernal and a couple other women picked up rocks and threw them at the car. Other picketers rushed the vehicle. Women in the hut and on the hillside joined them, pushing the car back down the road. The miners cheered. Inside the stroller, Angelina began to cry. Ana Maria picked up the baby and cradled her against her chest.

Sheriff Coleman strode up to the picket line. "Now listen here, ladies. I intend to clear this road. I don't want to arrest anybody, so I'm giving you a choice. You can go home, or you can go to jail."

"We have the right to march!" Señora Bernal yelled. "There's no injunction against us!"

"I've been ordered to clear this road," Coleman replied. He beckoned another car to come forward. The car rolled toward the scattered line of picketers. "So move aside!"

As the second vehicle drew closer, women lined up until their bodies formed a wall across the road.

Baby Angelina had stopped crying. Ana Maria started to lay her back in the stroller to check her diaper when movement on the side of the road caught her attention. Two scabs were trying to sneak around the women by climbing up through the gully.

"Look behind you!" Ana Maria shouted. Angelina flinched and began to wail.

Several women pounced on the scabs. A shiver of alarm ran through Ana Maria as she watched them tear at the men's hair and shove them back down the road.

Sheriff Coleman's face turned an angry red. "Violence will not be tolerated!"

He said something to two deputies. The men opened the trunk of a car. As they pulled out several red cylinders, Ana Maria's blood turned icy.

"Watch out!" shouted a miner. "That's tear gas."

Some women screamed and ran up the hill, while others froze. One of the deputies lobbed a cylinder into the center of the road. When the canister landed, white gas shot into the air.

Ana Maria grabbed the blanket from the stroller. She flung it over the wailing baby. The best path away from the gas was toward the arch. Ana Maria pressed the baby to her chest and ran.

As she reached the arch, Peter stepped into her path. "You can't go any farther. This is mine property."

James yanked Peter out of the way. "She has a baby. Do you want a baby gassed?"

"It's just a Mexican baby," Peter said.

James made a disgusted sound. He took Ana Maria by the shoulders and turned her to face the wooden beam of the arch. "Keep the baby down low." He gently pushed Ana Maria's head down. "Close your eyes."

Ana Maria hunched over the screaming, squirming Angelina. She felt James behind her, sheltering her from any chemicals the wind might blow their way.

But the wind drifted back toward the deputies.

"I think it's okay now," James said after a while.

Ana Maria opened her eyes and turned around. The sheriff and deputies had retreated, and the picketers were regrouping. Women were hauling large rocks into the road to prevent more cars from trying to break through the line.

Peter sneered. "That baby needs its diaper changed."

He was right, but Ana Maria ignored him. She touched James's elbow. "Thanks for helping me."

He nodded but looked away quickly. She understood. In an emergency, James would do the right thing, but he did not want her to think they were friends again.

"Ana Maria!" Señora Bernal stood among the women on the road. She motioned Ana Maria to bring Angelina to her.

"Ladies," Sheriff Coleman's voice boomed, "you were warned. Disturbing the peace, throwing rocks, unlawful assembly, assaulting deputies—pick your charge."

The deputies stepped into the crowd and began to haul women away. Anyone who resisted was handcuffed. The miners on the hill booed and jeered. Women shouted at the deputies in Spanish. Angelina wailed louder. Ana Maria sheltered the baby's head with one hand and pushed through the line to reach Señora Bernal. The woman's eyes were wide with alarm. She took Angelina, but before she could retreat to the hill, a deputy seized her by the arm.

"You're under arrest for throwing rocks," he said.

"Please!" Señora Bernal said. "I have a baby!"

"You should have thought of that before you threw those rocks." The deputy shoved her toward a police car.

Señora Bernal thrust Angelina toward Ana Maria. "Take her to my house. My husband is there!"

The deputy stepped between them, pushing the baby back into Señora Bernal's arms. He grabbed Ana Maria's elbow. "You're under arrest too."

"But I didn't do anything!" Ana Maria cried.

The deputy ignored her. Ana Maria looked desperately for Papá. He was already halfway down the hill, leaning forward as though prepared to launch himself into the air. But two miners held him back.

"Papá!" Ana Maria cried.

"Don't call him," Señora Bernal said in Spanish. "If the men get involved, they'll be violating the court order, and that means trouble."

Ana Maria pressed her lips together tight. The deputy shoved her into the back seat of his car, along with Señora Bernal, baby Angelina, and two women from Santa Rita.

As the deputy drove toward town, Ana Maria looked over her shoulder. Women were coming down the hill to fill the gaps in the picket line left by those being arrested. Angelina wailed.

Ana Maria wanted to wail, too, but she kept silent. The hope she had felt earlier was gone, replaced by that familiar tightness in her throat. Papá and the miners had tried to speak up for better treatment on the job. The company and the courts had silenced them. Today, the women had tried to speak up by marching. Now, they were going to jail. When people without power tried to use their voices, there was always a price to pay. It was safer to just keep quiet.

Chapter 7

The jail cell smelled like sweat and fear and dirty diaper. Ana Maria's legs ached. She longed to sit down, but the space was too packed with women and children. She stood against the concrete wall beside Señora Bernal and a woman who kept banging a tin cup against the cell bars. Each clang of metal against metal felt like a spike was being driven into Ana Maria's temples.

Two Anglo deputies sat in chairs outside the cell. One man had hair the color of a carrot, and the other had a nose shaped like an ax blade.

"I need to change Angelina's diaper," Señora Bernal said. Sweat trickled down her face.

"Lay her on the end of the bed." Ana Maria nodded toward the back of the cell where Señora Morano lay stretched out on the cot. The elderly woman had grown faint only minutes after the deputies locked them in.

The cell's only ventilation was a small grate above the bed. Hoping there might be more air back there, Ana Maria followed Señora Bernal between the crammed bodies to the bed. Señora Morano's face was ashen and shiny with sweat. Señora Bernal lay Angelina beside the old woman and quickly changed the baby's diaper.

"Give this to the deputies, por favor." Señora Bernal handed the rolled-up dirty cloth diaper to Ana Maria. "There's no way to rinse it out in here. They'll just have to throw it away."

Ana Maria swallowed hard and took the smelly bundle. Holding the diaper above her head, she made her way to the front of the cell. She thrust the diaper between the bars.

"Will you please throw this away?" she asked the deputies.

Carrot-head twisted his mouth in disgust. "I'm not touching that."

She stretched her arm out farther. "We can't keep it in here. It's too hot and crowded. People will get sick."

"That's what you get when you bring your babies to a picket line," he said.

Ana Maria's hand twitched. She wanted to lob the diaper at his head.

"You can't treat us like animals!" one woman yelled.

"We have rights!" shouted another.

The woman with the tin cup began banging again.

The pounding, the stench, the heat. Ana Maria's head throbbed. The deputy with the big nose walked down the hall and out a door. Carrot-head just yawned as if their complaints bored him.

Something inside her clicked. Cars plowing through the picket line. Tear gas spewing into the air. Peter saying, "It's just a Mexican baby." The cell door slamming shut. Now, this deputy ignoring her.

Ana Maria set the diaper on the floor outside the cell. "If I have to smell this any longer, I'm going to throw up. Then your jail will stink even worse than it already does."

With the flat of her hand, she whacked the diaper hard. It slid across the floor and hit the deputy's boot. He gave a little shout and lifted both feet into the air.

The woman with the cup cackled. "Are you afraid of a little baby poop?"

Carrot-head stood up. "Why you little—"

Just then the other deputy returned, carrying a paper bag. "Cool it, Jake," he said. "The girl is right. This thing stinks." He picked up the diaper, put it in the bag, and handed it to Carrot-head. "Go throw it in the dumpster."

Carrot-head glared at Ana Maria for a long moment. She did not look away. Then he grabbed the bag and stalked off.

Señora Talamante pushed her way to the bars. "We need food and water. Either feed us or release us."

The remaining deputy held up both hands. "I'm not in charge here."

"Then get somebody who is!" Juana yelled.

He disappeared back down the hall.

Ana Maria slumped against the bars. Minutes ticked by, and still no one came. Angelina began to fuss. Two little brothers whined that they were hungry. The women's conversations grew heavy with anger and fear.

"We're going to have to get noisy again," said the woman with the cup.

"It didn't work before," Señora Talamante said.

"How about we start a chant?" Mrs. Bradley suggested.

At that moment, one of the little boys cried, "Queremos comida."

"The niño nailed it!" Señora Talamante said. "Queremos comida. We want food."

"And drink," said another woman.

"And the bathroom," said a third.

Señora Talamante started the chant. "Queremos comida. Queremos bebidas. Queremos baños."

Everyone joined in. Their words bounced off the walls and echoed down the hall. Ana Maria's head throbbed in rhythm. She leaned her forehead against the cool metal of the iron bars and closed her eyes.

A few minutes later, an irritated Sheriff Coleman appeared with his two deputies. He held up both hands. "Listen, ladies. I'm willing to release you all, on one condition."

Hope rose in Ana Maria's chest. She would agree to anything to get out of here.

"You must promise to go straight home and not return to the picket line."

Cries of protest erupted. "No way!" shouted the woman with the cup.

Ana Maria's skull rattled. *I'll go straight home. I promise.* The words were on the tip of her tongue.

But Señora Talamante stood tall. With her chin up and her hair pinned in a braid on the top of her head, she looked like an Aztec queen. "We do not accept," she said. "When you release us, we'll return to the picket line. We are fighting for our dignity."

The women cheered and clapped.

Sheriff Coleman nodded, as if he was not surprised. "Have it your way. Enjoy your lunch, ladies."

The deputies passed paper cups of cold beans and slices of sandwich bread through the bars.

The shadows cast by the sun through the tiny window clocked the long hours. Finally, when the sky had turned to dusky pink, Sheriff Coleman returned. "Alright women, you're free to go."

Cheers erupted.

"For now," he clarified. "You'll be notified by mail of the date of your arraignment."

"What does that mean?" Ana Maria whispered to Señora Talamante.

"That's when we have to appear in court to be charged." Worry must have shown on Ana Maria's face because Señora Talamante patted her hand and said, "Don't worry. We'll plead not guilty, of course."

But Ana Maria did worry. She never wanted to see the inside of a jail cell again.

The living room was dark when she got home. Ana Maria was relieved that Papá had already gone to bed. She wanted to crawl under her covers and forget the day.

Then something clattered in the kitchen. Ana Maria gasped when she saw Papá standing at the sink. Not once in her life had she ever seen Papá wash dishes.

He turned to look at her, a dishrag in his hand.

"You're finally home. Good." He dropped the rag into the tub. "Finish these dishes." He walked past her into the living room and dropped down on the sofa.

"I'm so tired, Papá. I'll do them tomorrow." She turned toward her bedroom.

"No!" His command made her stop in her tracks. "Finish them now. If you're tired, it's your own fault. I told you to stay away from that picket line, and you went right into the thick of it. You directly disobeyed me. Again."

I was bringing a baby to her mother.

"Jail is no place for a young girl."

I did not choose to go to jail.

"Your place is here. At home. I had to eat cold ham and stale tortillas for supper tonight, thanks to you."

I had to eat cold beans and stale bread.

"If Javier wants Juana or Gabriela to picket, that's his decision, but you are my daughter." Papá shook his head. "Watching you hauled away today and knowing you were behind bars—I felt shame, Ana Maria. Shame."

Fear, Papá. I felt fear.

"I was powerless to help you."

I, too, was powerless.

But Ana Maria was too tired to voice her thoughts, and Papá would not listen anyway.

"Just like I couldn't help your mamá," he whispered.

Ana Maria started. Had she heard him correctly?

Before she could ask him to repeat himself, Papá stood. "Where's the vihuela? I found a buyer in Silver City, and I want to see what kind of condition it's in before I name a price."

Papá's words were a punch to the stomach. Ana Maria opened her mouth, but only a dry cough came out.

He waved a dismissive hand at her. "Ah, you can barely stand up. Go to bed. Tomorrow, you can finish the dishes and give me the vihuela."

In her bedroom, Ana Maria climbed into bed. Time was running out. She had not made any money to give Papá. She had not finished writing the corrido for Mamá. But the corrido would mean nothing if she didn't have a vihuela to play it on.

Entonces Teresa se unió a otras mujeres
Cuyo sueño también fue atrapado.
Marcharon. Bailaron. Se enfrentaron.
Pero todo fue infundado.

El monstruo arrasó contra ellos,
Con sus garras y afilados colmillos.
Los capturó en su calabozo
Y los encerró entre cadenas.

★ TALENT ★
★ SHOW ★

Ten CASH PRIZES range from $5 to $50

Competition open to all ages

Performance on Saturday, July 21

Western College, Silver City

Doors open at 6:30

Performances begin at 7:30

Audition on July 5 or 6 in Light Hall

Chapter 8

When Ana Maria reached Zinke's grocery store, the sign on the front window caught her eye. As she read it, the hair on her arms stood up in excitement.

Cash prizes! She stepped inside the store, her mind racing as she headed toward the eggs. If she performed her corrido and won a prize, she could give the money to Papá so he wouldn't have to sell her vihuela.

But July 21 was less than a month away. She still had to finish writing the corrido and then practice until she was perfect. Was there time?

Ana Maria grabbed a carton of eggs and headed for the checkout. The bell on the door jingled, and James, Peter, and Larry entered the store. They headed for the candy rack. Larry smiled at Ana Maria, but James did not look at her. Peter wore his usual smirk.

Linda Bradley, the union organizer's daughter, was in the checkout line with a basket of groceries. "Hey, Ana Maria," she said. "Wasn't that wild yesterday?"

Ana Maria nodded. "It was awful."

Linda's blue eyes widened. "I thought it was exciting. How many kids our age can say they have gone to jail to battle injustice?"

"Battle injustice?" The cashier's voice was heavy with scorn. "Is that what your communist parents call it?"

A flush crept up Linda's neck. "My parents aren't communists."

Ana Maria frowned. There was that word again. *Communism.*

The Anglo cashier clicked her tongue. "That's not what I heard. Everybody got along around here. Miners and farmers. Whites and Mexicans. Then your folks moved to town and stirred everything up with their communism."

"Yeah," Peter called from the next aisle. "If you jailbirds like communism so much, why don't you move to Russia?"

Ana Maria glared at Peter. James pulled Larry toward the magazine rack.

"That will be three dollars and seventy-eight cents," the cashier said.

Linda said, "Please put it on my parents'—"

"In cash," the woman interrupted.

Linda's blush deepened. "Can't you put it on my parents' account?"

"Nope." The cashier bit off the word. "No more credit to strikers. If you want groceries, you've got to pay up front."

Linda turned to Ana Maria, a plea on her face. Ana Maria held out her palm to show one dime, two nickels, and four pennies. "Sorry. I only have enough for a dozen eggs."

Linda turned back to the cashier. "Well, I guess you'll have to put all these things back on the shelves then." She lifted her chin, dropped her basket on the counter, and strode out the door.

In the other aisle, Peter snickered. Ana Maria shot another glare at him.

The cashier rang up Ana Maria's eggs, all the while studying her suspiciously through bullet-shaped eyes. Ana Maria put her coins down on the counter and scurried out the door as quickly as she could.

Out on the sidewalk, Ana Maria ran to catch up with Linda. "That woman was not very nice."

"She was awful," Linda said. "My parents are going to be steaming mad that Zinke's won't let strikers buy on credit anymore."

Ana Maria knew that without store credit, Papá would be even more anxious to sell her vihuela. That morning, he had examined every scratch on the instrument and plucked each string. At least he had given the vihuela back to her after he had inspected it.

"Peter Long is a jerk too," Linda said.

"He's so mean."

"'If your parents like communism so much, why don't they move to Russia?'" Linda mocked Peter's voice. "He doesn't know anything about anything."

"I don't even know what communism is," Ana Maria said. "But everybody seems terrified of it."

"They shouldn't be," Linda said. "It's just an economic system."

Ana Maria stumbled on a section of broken sidewalk. Even her body felt confused this morning. "I don't know what that means. And why was Peter talking about Russia?"

"Because Peter is a fool," Linda said. "Most Americans think anyone who is communist must love Russia because Russia has a communist government."

Ana Maria frowned. "And why's that bad?"

"Well, Joseph Stalin is the leader of Russia. Basically, he's a dictator. If you disagree with him?" Linda ran her finger across her neck in a slicing motion.

Ana Maria drew back. "Killed?"

Linda nodded. "Pretty much. Heck, Stalin would probably love to blow the United States into a million pieces if he could get away with it."

Alarm ran through Ana Maria. "Well, no wonder everybody hates communism. It sounds awful!"

They had reached the railroad tracks, the dividing line in Alba. Turning left led to the white neighborhood, while a right turn led to the Mexican American community. Both girls turned right.

The Bradleys were different from other Anglos. When they'd arrived in Alba, they'd moved into the Mexican American neighborhood. Most union members were Mexican American, and Scott Bradley wanted his family to live among the people he worked for.

Linda waved one hand in the air as if to erase what she had just said. "I'm explaining it wrong. Communist ideas are good. Well, some of them anyway. It's the way the Russian government carries out these ideas that's bad."

None of this made sense to Ana Maria. What she wanted to know was whether Papá was a communist.

"You know what?" Linda faced Ana Maria. "My mom can explain this way better than I can. Come with us to Bayard this afternoon. We're working on donation letters."

"What's a donation letter?"

"We're sending requests to unions around the country asking them to send money to help the strikers pay their bills. Come help us, and then my mom can explain what communism means."

Donations might mean Papá would not have to sell her vihuela. And he could not object to her stuffing envelopes. That was a girl's job.

"Okay," Ana Maria said. "I'll come."

Sunlight streamed through the windows of the union hall, casting a warm glow over the banner that hung by the American flag.

"That," Mrs. Bradley said, pointing to the banner, "is a key principle in the Mine-Mill constitution. It's also a communist principle. Do you understand it?"

Ana Maria read the banner out loud. "'An injury to one is an injury to all.' Well, does it mean if something hurts me, then it hurts you too?"

"That's right," Mrs. Bradley said. "The theory of communism is about empowering working people."

Ana Maria screwed up her mouth as she studied the banner. "I still don't get it. If I fall down and break my leg,

I'm hurt. But Linda's leg is fine. So how does my injury hurt her?"

"Think about it this way," Mrs. Bradley said. "What if Empire Zinc refused to put support beams in a tunnel, and when your dad was in the mine, the wall caved in and broke his leg?"

A shiver of unease ran up Ana Maria's spine. Last year, a miner had been killed in a cave-in.

Mrs. Bradley continued. "He's injured, but the rest of the miners aren't. Should they just pull your dad out and go back to work?"

"Of course not."

"Why not? After all, the other men weren't injured."

"Because it could happen to them," Ana Maria said. "If the tunnel wall isn't strengthened, another miner could get injured."

Mrs. Bradley snapped her fingers. "Bingo. An injury to one is an injury to all. We have to have solidarity. That means we have to stick together. Workers have more power when they speak with one voice. That's what the union is. The voice of united miners."

"And that's communism?"

"Wellll." Mrs. Bradley stretched the word out. "Not exactly. Communism is more complicated. The part that makes people nervous is that communists believe true economic justice won't happen until the working class overthrows the rich."

Linda chimed in. "Like the Russian Revolution of 1917."

Ana Maria's eyes widened. "A revolution? Like a war?"

Mrs. Bradley shook her head. "That's what happened in Russia, but we're not fighting a physical war here. We're fighting a moral war. Think about it." She patted Ana Maria's hand. "What happened to your mom could happen to any of us." She gestured to the other women in the hall. "None of us has hot water or a gas stove. We aren't fighting for communism. We're fighting for basic human dignity."

Mrs. Bradley stood up and smiled down at Ana Maria. "And isn't that what everyone deserves?" She walked off to join women at another table.

Linda raised her eyebrows and grimaced. "Sorry. My mom goes overboard sometimes."

"No, it was helpful," Ana Maria said. "I understand communism better now, although I still don't get why people get so mad about it."

Linda shrugged. "People are strange."

As Ana Maria folded letters and stuffed them into envelopes, the words played over and over in her mind. *Communism. Broken bones. Basic human dignity.*

That night, Ana Maria paused before entering her bedroom. Papá lay on the couch reading the newspaper. His anger about her arrest had faded. Ana Maria felt she could ask the question that had been worrying her all day.

"Papá, are you a communist?"

He lowered the paper and looked at her. "A communist? What makes you ask that?"

"I was just wondering. The woman at the grocery store this morning called the Bradleys communists."

Papá snorted. "No, mija. I'm not a communist. Unless a communist is someone who wants to be treated fairly even though his skin is brown and he can speak Spanish."

A smile crept across his face. "If that's the case, I guess I'm a communist."

As Ana Maria prepared for bed, she reflected on Papá's words. He and the other strikers were fighting for dignity and justice. Like the women, the miners were also fighting to be heard. As Ana Maria drifted off to sleep, more words to the corrido rose in the corners of her mind. She had to remember to write the words down tomorrow. So she could practice her song. Win the talent show. Save her vihuela.

Teresa examinó la oscura celda
Para su sorpresa sus ojos vieran
Atrapados bajo tierra y sin voz
Hombres con ojos de mineros eran.

Los hombres debilitados teñidos de negro por la tierra
Sosteniendo el zinc azul plateada.
Su amada la miró enmudecida
Pues su alma también había sido silenciada.

Chapter 9

Ana Maria paced back and forth across the living room. Papá had left for Silver City. Today was the first hearing on his charge for disturbing the peace back in June. Soon, Papá would face a hostile judge, and the women on the picket line would face hostile deputies. What would Ana Maria face today? Nothing but housework.

She could not stand it a second longer. She ran out the front door, through the gate, and onto the road. She faced north, toward the mine. The sky was blue, but here and there gray clouds punched through, as if somewhere a storm was warming up for a fight.

At the sound of footsteps, Ana Maria turned. Gabriela was coming up the road.

"Are you ready?" her friend called. "We can get a ride with Mrs. Bradley."

"A ride where?"

"The picket line, of course. Didn't your papá tell you? Everyone is needed for marching today."

This morning, Papá had barely spoken. "No, he didn't," Ana Maria said. "Papá doesn't want me anywhere near the picket line. He says it isn't a proper place for women."

"So you aren't coming?" Gabriela drew back in disbelief. "But they need us today. My mamá is there. I bet yours would be, too, if she could."

Ana Maria considered this. If Mamá were still alive, Papá would not want her to march. But would Mamá have defied him and marched anyway? Ana Maria was almost certain the answer was yes.

She looked at the house. Weeds were creeping into the vegetable garden. Thirsty tomato plants were wilting. Split firewood lay around the woodpile. Then her gaze fell on the ax. It leaned casually against a stump.

Her blood began to boil. Because of Empire Zinc and that ax, Mamá never got to choose whether to march or not.

Ana Maria strode to the stump, picked up the ax with both hands, and, roaring like a lion, threw it as hard as she could. The ax was so heavy that it landed only a foot away. Still, it felt good to throw it.

Today she would march. For Mamá.

When Ana Maria turned around, Gabriela was staring at her with a look that was half alarm and half amusement.

Ana Maria dusted off her hands and smiled. "What are we waiting for?"

The weapons were laid out on the picnic table in the picketers' hut. Straight pins. Small rocks. Little brown paper sacks filled with cayenne pepper.

"Fill your pockets," Señora Talamante told the teenagers gathered around the table. Twenty young people had shown up. Gabriela and Ana Maria were the youngest. "Be careful with the pepper. It burns."

Unease crept up Ana Maria's spine. She had come to march for miners' rights, not to hurt anyone. Still, she slipped a sack of pepper into her pocket.

Mexican American and Anglo miners lined the hillside as if it were a sports stadium. One white man stood apart from the others. He wore pressed trousers and a plaid, button-down shirt. Ana Maria wondered if Empire Zinc had planted a spy among the strikers.

A dozen women marched in a circle across the road. Sheriff Coleman and his deputies formed a huddle about thirty feet back from the picket line. Cars and trucks full of scabs lined the road. Under the mine entrance arch stood several Empire Zinc executives, including Mr. Wagner. But James was not there.

Ana Maria and Gabriela sat with the teenagers at the bottom of the hill. They were allowed to join the picket line in pairs. By midmorning, it was Ana Maria and Gabriela's turn.

Gabriela's brown eyes sparkled. "I can't believe we're doing this!"

Ana Maria forced a smile. The fury she had felt earlier had vanished. Now she just felt vulnerable and nervous. As she walked, she kept her eyes on the feet of the woman in front of her.

They had only made a few passes of the road when someone shouted, "Here come the scabs. Line up!"

Ana Maria raised her head. A caravan of cars drove their way. She and Gabriela quickly fell in line with the other picketers. They stood shoulder to shoulder and faced the oncoming vehicles. The car in front seemed to be driving too fast.

Ana Maria swallowed. Her mouth was suddenly as dry as sand. Gabriela grabbed her hand.

Time distorted. Everything froze.

Sound was muffled as though she had cotton stuffed in her ears. The car came toward them like a monstrous beige beetle. The headlights were its bulbous eyes and the grille its grinning jaws.

Then everything sped up.

The car slammed into Gabriela, ripping Ana Maria's hand from her friend's grasp as Gabriela fell to the ground.

Sound came rushing back. Shrieks and shouts pierced the air. Ana Maria dropped to her knees beside her friend. Gabriela's face was twisted in pain. "He ran right into me," she cried. "Why did he run into me?"

Suddenly, Señora Talamante was there, cradling Gabriela's head in her arms. Someone pulled Ana Maria away. "Let the adults tend to her," a woman said.

Ana Maria rose on shaky legs. Women had surrounded the car and were pushing and shoving it so that it rocked. Ana Maria kicked at one of its headlights. Pain shot up her leg. She wanted to blind this beast.

The mob wrestled the car doors open, pulling the driver out. The man wore a deputy's uniform. His cowboy hat fell off, revealing a thatch of orange hair. It was Carrot-head.

"Were you trying to kill that little girl?" shrieked one woman as she grabbed him by his shirt.

The rage that had filled Ana Maria's blood earlier flooded back. Empire Zinc had already taken Mamá from her. They could not take Gabriela too! She plunged her hand into her pocket and pulled out the sack of pepper.

Ana Maria darted into the swarm that buzzed around the deputy. Ducking under a woman's arm, she came face-to-face with Carrot-head. He hunched over, fists raised, his mouth in a snarl. Ana Maria ripped open the paper sack and shook the pepper into his face.

"What the heck?" Carrot-head sputtered. He stumbled backward, his hands over his face. "My eyes! She blinded me!"

Ana Maria immediately dropped the paper bag and backed out of the angry circle. The pepper would not blind Carrot-head, but she did not want to get arrested again. Breathing hard and covered in sweat, Ana Maria stumbled around looking for Gabriela. She finally found her in the hut. Gabriela was sitting at the picnic table, her right leg propped up on her father's lap.

Ana Maria leaned close. "Are you okay?"

"Don't cry, Ana Maria," Gabriela said. "I'll be alright."

"I'm not crying."

"Tears are streaming down your cheeks."

"I threw pepper in that deputy's face," Ana Maria said. "I must have gotten some in my eyes."

"Good for you," said Señor Talamante. "I'd like to throw a fist in that man's face."

"Are you sure you're okay?" Ana Maria repeated.

"We don't think anything is broken," said Señora Talamante. "But we're taking her to the doctor, just in case."

After the Talamantes left, Ana Maria sat down on the bench. Eventually, her tears eased. She saw that a double line of women now blocked the road, at least forty strong. They stood like soldiers guarding a command post.

The well-dressed Anglo man that she had noticed earlier entered the hut. He sat down at the picnic table and smiled. "Hi. My name is Michael Wilson."

"Hello." Ana Maria eyed him suspiciously.

"I hope your friend is okay," he said.

The memory of Gabriela's hand being ripped from hers sent a shudder running through her.

"You two are the youngest picketers I've seen here today. Can I ask you a few questions about the strike?"

Ana Maria frowned. "Do you work for Empire Zinc?"

The man laughed. "No, I'm a screenwriter."

"What's that?"

"I write scripts for movies. I used to work in Hollywood."

Her eyebrows shot up. "Really?"

"Really," Mr. Wilson said. "Some folks want to make a movie about what's happening in Alba. They hired me to write the screenplay, so I'm here doing research."

"Why do you want to make a movie about Alba?"

"Not the town. We want to make a movie about the strike."

Ana Maria narrowed her eyes. This white man looked too much like the company bosses. "You mean a movie about how great the Empire Zinc Company is?"

Mr. Wilson laughed again. "You're smart to be suspicious. Actually, we want to tell the miners' story, because nobody in Hollywood will touch a story like this."

"Why not?"

He sighed. "Nowadays, when anyone mentions workers' rights, they're immediately labeled a communist."

There it was again. That word.

"Then aren't you afraid you'll be called a communist if you make a movie about this?" Ana Maria gestured toward the picket line.

Mr. Wilson's laugh was bitter. "Too late for that. I've already been blacklisted."

"What's *blacklisted*?"

"A few years ago, Congress investigated the movie industry. Politicians thought some of us were making movies that were too sympathetic to communists. Some of us producers, directors, and screenwriters refused to go along with the hearings. Now the movie production companies won't hire us. That's blacklisted."

"You should have just answered the politicians' questions," Ana Maria said. "Then you could have kept making movies."

Mr. Wilson shook his head. "But then we couldn't make the kinds of movies we think are important. The government wants to control the ideas and issues we explore. They want to stifle our voices."

Ana Maria turned to look directly at him. He was being silenced too.

"A bunch of us formed our own movie production company," Mr. Wilson continued. "We don't need Hollywood. I'm here to figure out how to tell the miners' story so we can put it on the big screen."

Ana Maria considered this. "So a screenwriter is basically a storyteller?"

He smiled. "Exactly."

Ana Maria had the urge to tell Mr. Wilson about her corrido. She had not told anyone yet. Not even Gabriela. But this man might understand, one storyteller to another.

Just then Mrs. Bradley entered the hut. "Ana Maria, I'm making a run back to town. Did you need a ride home?" She glanced at her watch. "I imagine your father will be back from Silver City soon."

Panic seized Ana Maria. If Papá came home and discovered she had gone to the picket line, there would be trouble. She jumped up. "Yes, please."

"I wanted to ask you some questions about how the strike is affecting your family," Mr. Wilson said.

Ana Maria gave him an apologetic shrug. "Sorry, I have to go."

He rose and extended his hand. "Tell me your name at least."

She shook his hand. "Ana Maria Carranza Garcia."

"It was nice to meet you. Will you be back on the picket line again?"

Ana Maria started to say no. Papá forbade it, and it was too dangerous. But she hesitated. Scores of women stood on the hill, waiting for their turn on the picket line. Some of them must have men in their lives who did not want them to march. Some of them must have felt as frightened as she had felt today. Yet here they were. Day after day. Marching for dignity.

"Yes," she said. "I don't know when, but I'll be back."

Chapter 10

Over the next several days, the temperature climbed—and so did Ana Maria's anxiety. The strike slogged on. Rent was due August 1. The talent show was on July 21. The clock ticked down.

But every day, Ana Maria took time to visit Gabriela. Her friend's spirits were low because she was stuck at home. The blow from the car had bruised Gabriela's right leg from hip to knee and sprained her right ankle. So Ana Maria played cards, read books, and chatted with her friend each afternoon.

Ana Maria also kept her vow to Mr. Wilson. On three occasions when Papá had business in Silver City, she went to the picket line with Linda and Mrs. Bradley. She took her turn marching but refused to carry pins, rocks, or red pepper. She saw Mr. Wilson talking to the miners. He waved to her, but they did not speak again.

In the rest of her spare time, Ana Maria worked on her corrido. She smoothed out every rough measure. She practiced chords until her fingers moved with a mind of their own. She controlled the rhythm as if it were her own breath. She played with words until the lyrics practically sang themselves. Deep in her heart, she thought maybe she was good enough to win first place.

But Ana Maria still had two big problems. First, how was she going to get to Silver City on the evening of the show? She could not ask Papá. How many times had he told her only men could be corridistos?

Second, she still had not settled on the corrido's final words. She had written a dozen versions, but none felt right. She did not know how to end her story.

The Tuesday evening before the talent show, Ana Maria was mulling over both these problems while washing dishes. There was a knock on the front door. Papá answered it. Ana Maria heard the familiar voice of Javier Talamante.

"This is Michael Wilson," Señor Talamante said. "He wants to interview you about the strike."

Fear shot through Ana Maria.

"Mucho gusto, Señor," Papá said. "Come in."

Ana Maria looked frantically around the narrow kitchen. If Mr. Wilson saw her, he was sure to say something about her being on the picket line. Papá would be furious. She flattened herself against the wall between the stove and the water barrel, out of sight of the living room.

For several minutes, Mr. Wilson asked Papá about his work at the mine and his complaints against Empire Zinc. As they chatted, Ana Maria began to relax.

Then Mr. Wilson said, "While I'm here, do you mind if I ask your daughter a few questions?"

A pit of dread opened in Ana Maria's stomach.

"Why do you want to talk to my daughter?" Papá said.

"Well, she's the youngest person I've seen on the picket line, and I'd like to know what motivates her to march."

The room fell quiet. The silence stretched out, pulling Ana Maria's nerves almost to the point of snapping.

Papá finally replied. "I'd like to know what motivates her too."

She squeezed her eyes shut.

"Ana Maria, vete aquí!" Papá barked.

She dragged herself into the living room. Señor Tala-mante sat in the rocking chair. He shot her a look of regret. Papá and Mr. Wilson sat at opposite ends of the sofa.

"Siéntate!" Papá ordered.

Ana Maria pulled over a chair from the table and sat in front of the couch.

Mr. Wilson must have sensed the sudden tension because his smile was uncertain. "Hello, Ana Maria. It's good to see you again."

"Hello." Her voice was barely above a whisper.

"Remind me." Papá leaned forward, resting his elbows on his knees. He pinned Ana Maria in place with his stare. "How did you and Mr. Wilson meet?"

"It was on July 11," Mr. Wilson answered. "The day everything went crazy at the picket line."

"July 11." Papá nodded. "The day I was in court." An angry red flush was creeping up his neck. Ana Maria looked down at her hands twisted together in her lap.

"Do you mind answering a few questions for me, Ana Maria?" Mr. Wilson asked.

She glanced at Papá. He smiled tightly and nodded. "Okay," she said.

"Why do you march?" Mr. Wilson asked. "What do you hope to accomplish?"

"You mean why did she march, don't you?" Papá interjected. "On July 11, the one time you met."

Mr. Wilson frowned. "Well, yes. I want to know why she marched that day, but also why she continues to march." He turned to Ana Maria. "Didn't I see you on the picket line just yesterday?"

Ana Maria closed her eyes briefly. "Yes, I have marched a few times."

Papá leaned back and crossed his arms. He was a wall of anger.

"You're young and it's summer vacation," Mr. Wilson said. "What draws you to the picket line when you could be out playing with your friends?"

"Well . . . um . . ."

Papá clapped his hands together. The noise made them all jump.

"Calm, Martín," Señor Talamante said softly.

"Answer the question," Papá said through clenched teeth. "Why have you been going to the picket line?"

Outside, the wind groaned. Ana Maria felt the sound in her soul. Suddenly, she felt very sad. The anger she saw in Papá's eyes made her own fill with tears. "I march for Mamá."

Papá flinched.

"For your mother?" Mr. Wilson leaned forward.

"Yes," Ana Maria said. "I march for my mother because she is not here to march for herself."

Papá drew breath in a sharp hiss. But he had demanded that she answer Mr. Wilson's questions, and she was determined to finish. If only she could find the right words to make Papá understand why she had disobeyed him.

"Mamá told me to follow my dreams. But she never had a chance to do that herself. I think if Mamá were alive, she would be on that picket line. So I march for her."

Outside, the wind moaned, but inside no one said a word for a long time.

"I'm very sorry about your mother," Mr. Wilson finally said. "May I ask how she died?"

Ignoring the tightness in her throat, Ana Maria said, "The company refuses to put indoor plumbing in our houses. Every day, Mamá had to chop wood to heat water. One day, she slipped and cut her foot. It got infect—"

Papá stood up. "It's late, Mr. Wilson. Time to say goodnight."

The man looked up in surprise. He gestured to Ana Maria. "But the interview—"

"Is over." Papá walked to the front door and opened it. "Good evening."

Mr. Wilson turned to Señor Talamante, who just shrugged. Then he went to Ana Maria and shook her hand. "Thanks for speaking with me." He leaned closer and whispered, "Sorry if I've stirred up trouble."

She gave him a weak smile. The men left, and Papá returned to the living room. He dropped onto the couch with a heavy sigh and stared at her. His face was a mixture of disappointment and anger.

"You're wrong, you know," he finally said. "Your mother respected my opinion."

Ana Maria held her tongue.

"If I said I didn't want her on the picket line, she would not have gone."

Still Ana Maria said nothing.

Papá pointed a finger at her. "That's the difference between you and your mother. Respect."

The words exploded out of Ana Maria's mouth. "You didn't even know Mamá had written a letter to Empire Zinc! How can you be so sure she would not have marched with the other women?"

"Don't tell me that I didn't know my wife." Papá leaned forward. "I knew Teresa. I knew her. It's you that I'm starting to think I don't know."

Tears stung the backs of Ana Maria's eyes, but she blinked them away. "You're right, Papá. You don't know me. I'm sorry you're disappointed in me, but I'm not sorry I marched." She lifted her chin. "You always tell me to do the *proper* thing. Well, I decided to do the *right* thing instead."

Papá leaned back as if to get a better look at her. Then he let out a frustrated laugh. "Do you also think it's the *right* thing to tell Mr. Wilson, this complete stranger, the story of your mother's death?" His voice cracked on the last word. "He wants to make a movie about us. Do you want our pain plastered over the big screen? I know you blame me, but would you hurt me like that?"

Ana Maria blinked. "Blame you? Blame you for what?"

"For your mother's death, of course!" Papá shouted. "You tell everyone how she died. You told the union meeting. You tell this Mr. Wilson. I didn't chop wood for my wife. I didn't take my wife to the doctor in time." He dropped his head into his hands.

She stared at him, her mouth open. "I don't blame you, Papá. I never have. I blame Empire Zinc."

He lifted his head. "Well, you should blame me." His voice sounded like it had been scraped out of him. "Your mother's death *was* my fault. I was her husband. I should have chopped the wood. I should have taken her to the doctor right away. It *was* my fault."

He rose and slowly walked into his bedroom, his shoulders hunched like he was carrying the weight of the world.

Ana Maria sat for a long time. The wind quieted down, and the moon shone through the window. When she finally stood up, she thought she understood something important about Papá. After Mamá died, while Ana Maria had turned her anger outward onto Empire Zinc, Papá had turned his anger inward onto himself.

Taking down the ofrenda. Returning the record console. Refusing to discuss Mamá. It was not that Papá wanted to forget his wife because he did not love her or miss her. It was because the memory of how she'd died came with so much guilt.

Ana Maria crawled into bed, but sleep refused to come. Eventually, she got up and retrieved her vihuela from under the bed. Propping herself against the wall, she quietly strummed and sang. When she fell asleep two hours later, she had finally figured out an ending to the corrido.

Chapter 11

The next morning, the sky was gray and orange. Papá was silent over breakfast. After he shoveled the last bit of egg and tortilla into his mouth, he said, "The man who is interested in the vihuela is coming on Sunday morning. Have it tuned and polished."

"But—"

"I know, I know," Papá said wearily. "How can you play your corridos without the vihuela?" He met her gaze. "Last night, you told Mr. Wilson that your mother wanted you to follow your dreams. Well, your father"—he slapped his chest—"wants you to stop living in a dream world and face reality. If you are old enough to walk the picket line, you're also old enough to accept that sacrifices must be made to pay the rent."

Papá left for the picket line. Ana Maria's mind raced as she washed the breakfast dishes. The corrido was complete.

She just needed a ride to Silver City on Saturday. But everyone Ana Maria knew with a car was a friend of Papá's. If Papá found out she intended to sing onstage, he would forbid it. Ana Maria did not want Papá to know anything about the talent show until she could hand him the prize money.

In her bedroom, Ana Maria sat down at the dresser to fix her hair. The dresser top was covered with hair ribbons, crayons, and root beer candies. Dragging a brush through her hair, Ana Maria looked at the root beer candies. Why did she have them? She hated root beer. Then she remembered. Mrs. Wagner had given her the candies as a consolation prize for losing the spelling bee.

An idea took hold in Ana Maria's mind. Mrs. Wagner knew Papá, but they were not friends and rarely saw each other. Ana Maria quickly plunked her brush down on the dresser. There was no time to waste.

The curtains on the windows of the Wagners' house were pulled back. But the sun glinting off the glass made it impossible to see inside. In the tree beside the house, a desert cardinal whistled. *Ready, set, go*, the bird seemed to cry. Ana Maria steeled her courage and rapped on the door.

A second later, James opened it. His eyebrows shot up in surprise at the sight of her.

"Hi, James," she said. "Is your mom home?"

He frowned. "Why do you want to see my mom?"

"I just need to ask her something."

His frown changed to a look of curiosity, and he stepped back to let her in.

Ana Maria slipped off her chanclas and followed James through the living room. Comic books were scattered on the couch. A basket of laundry sat on a recliner. Two dirty glasses and an empty bowl seemed forgotten on a side table. The living room had never looked like this when Mamá had worked here.

James pushed through the swinging door into the kitchen. Ana Maria followed. Her eyes widened when she saw the mess.

A tower of dishes tilted dangerously in the sink. Mixing bowls, measuring cups, and spice containers covered the table. Flour dusted the counter. Mrs. Wagner was facing the stove, but she turned when they entered. Ana Maria had to hold back a giggle. A streak of dough ran down Mrs. Wagner's cheek.

"Ana Maria!" Mrs. Wagner stepped forward and enveloped her in an embrace.

"Mom, you're a mess," James said.

"Whoops." Mrs. Wagner laughed and plucked a fleck of dough off Ana Maria's forehead. "You'll never guess what I'm making."

"Trying to make," James muttered.

"Buñuelos! I woke up with such a craving for them." Mrs. Wagner patted Ana Maria's cheek with a sticky palm. "Your mother used to make the most delicious buñuelos. I'm trying to follow her recipe, but . . ." She gestured to a plate holding a stack of black discs. "I really miss your mother's cooking. I lack her talent."

"That's for sure," James said.

"Oh shush." She shooed her son.

James waved one hand in the air. "It stinks in here. I'm going to go read."

"That is no way to treat your guest," Mrs. Wagner said.

"She's here to see you, Mom," he said over his shoulder.

Mrs. Wagner gave Ana Maria a wide-eyed look. "To see me? How lovely."

Suddenly, Ana Maria's confidence vanished. "Well, uh, I was wondering . . ." This had been a stupid idea. Mrs. Wagner wouldn't want to drive her to Silver City. Papá was a striker and James's father was a supervisor for Empire Zinc. Their families were on opposite sides in this fight. "Never mind. You're busy and it's not important."

"Oh, don't go," Mrs. Wagner said. She picked up one of the charred buñuelos and snapped it in half. Black crumbs drifted to the floor. "Did you ever help your mother make these?"

"Lots of times."

Mrs. Wagner clasped her hands to her chest. "Will you help me? Please! Before I burn down the house?"

Ana Maria glanced at the clock over the kitchen window. It was only midmorning. She could help Mrs. Wagner for a little while and still have time to figure out how to get a ride to Silver City.

An hour later, the dishes were washed, the table clean, and the floor swept. Ana Maria and Mrs. Wagner sat across from each other at the table, munching crisp, golden buñuelos dusted with sugar.

"Delicious." Mrs. Wagner fluttered her eyelids. Then she leaned forward. "Now, my dear, please tell me why you came to see me." Ana Maria started to shake her head, but Mrs. Wagner continued. "Please, I know you need something. Let me help you."

Setting her buñuelo down on the plate, Ana Maria wiped her mouth with her hand. What did she have to lose? "I need a ride to Silver City on Saturday night."

Mrs. Wagner sat back. "That's it?"

Ana Maria nodded. "Well, a ride there and back."

"What time?"

"I have to be at Western College by six thirty."

"What's at Western?"

Ana Maria hesitated. So far, she hadn't told anyone about the talent show. But she wanted *someone* to know that on Saturday, in front of a panel of judges, she would be telling the story of her community's pain. And her own.

"I wrote a song that I'm going to perform in the talent show," she said.

Mrs. Wagner clapped her hands. "How marvelous! I'd be happy to drive you. Will your father be joining us?"

"No," Ana Maria said quickly. "He can't make it. But—are you sure?"

"Of course!" Mrs. Wagner said. "Let's see, we'd need to leave here around six. When should I pick you up?"

Ana Maria could just imagine Papá looking out the window and wondering why the Wagners' shiny red Chevrolet was parked out front. She stood up and set her plate in the sink. "You don't have to pick me up. I'll meet you here a little before six."

Mrs. Wagner walked Ana Maria to the door and hugged her. "It's been so nice to see you. I miss your mother every day around here. Every single day."

Mrs. Wagner was nice, and Ana Maria was grateful to her. But, as her eyes fell on the dirty tracks on the carpet, she could not help but wonder if it was Mamá that Mrs. Wagner missed or the work Mamá had done for her.

Ana Maria stepped out onto the front porch.

Mrs. Wagner called after her, "What's the song about? The one you're going to sing for the show?"

Ana Maria hesitated. How could she explain her corrido to Mrs. Wagner? When they had fried the buñuelos, Mrs. Wagner had not needed to chop wood to heat the stove. When they cleaned up, Mrs. Wagner had not needed to get water from an outdoor pump. All around Ana Maria was the injustice at the heart of her ballad.

She shrugged. "It's about life on the Mexican American side of town."

"Oh really. What's the song's title?"

"It's called 'The Miners' Lament.'"

A tiny pucker of uncertainty appeared between Mrs. Wagner's eyebrows.

"I'll see you on Saturday just before six. Thanks again." Ana Maria headed home before the woman could change her mind.

Chapter 12

*A*na Maria needed Gabriela's help to escape the house on Saturday evening without rousing Papá's suspicions. So, she finally told Gabriela about how Papá planned to sell her vihuela and how she planned to save it. After being mad about not being told sooner, Gabriela rubbed her hands together and hatched a plot.

As luck would have it, the Talamantes had business in Bayard on Saturday evening and would not be home until late. Meanwhile, Papá had agreed to help Señor Torrez, the union president, repair his roof. On Saturday morning, Ana Maria asked Papá if she could sleep at Gabriela's house that night to help her babysit. He agreed.

Late Saturday afternoon, Ana Maria put on a blue-flowered cotton dress and black patent leather shoes. She slipped her notebook into her pocket and her vihuela case over her shoulder, and headed toward Zinc Hill Road.

When she knocked on the Wagners' door twenty minutes later, her heart was galloping in her chest.

Mrs. Wagner opened the door. "You're right on time." She looked over Ana Maria's shoulder. "No friends to cheer you on tonight?"

"Nope." Ana Maria smiled nervously. "Just me."

"Well, that won't do. Just give me a minute." She disappeared into the kitchen.

The Wagners' living room was as messy as it had been the other day. James's voice drifted through the closed kitchen door. Ana Maria could not make out the words, but he did not sound happy.

A minute later, Mrs. Wagner emerged, with a scowling James on her heels. "Look who's coming," she said. "Friends should support each other."

James gave Ana Maria a look that said this was all her fault.

On the drive to Silver City, nervous sweat dripped down Ana Maria's sides, but her fingers were icicles. She paged through her notebook, reviewing each verse of the corrido. Finally, they arrived at the college.

Inside Light Hall, Mrs. Wagner walked briskly toward the auditorium, where an official was checking in the performers at a table. Ana Maria followed, dragging her feet. She felt like she might throw up.

James asked, "Are you nervous?"

Ana Maria tried to smile. "Terrified."

When they reached the table, the official was reviewing his list. He frowned up at Mrs. Wagner. "What did you say the name was again?"

"Ana Maria Carranza Garcia." Mrs. Wagner pulled Ana Maria forward. "Here she is."

The official frowned. "I'm sorry, but that name isn't here." He looked at Ana Maria. "Did you audition?"

Dread descended on Ana Maria as suddenly as if someone had thrown a blanket over her head. "Audition?"

The official winced. "Oh, I'm sorry. Didn't you know that you had to audition?" He held up a copy of the flyer she had seen in the grocery store last month. On the last line were the words "Audition on July 5 or 6 in Light Hall."

"If we didn't have auditions," the official said, "we'd have too many performers."

Ana Maria's shoulders slumped. The strap of the vihuela case slid off her arm.

James caught the case before it could fall, and he pushed the strap back up Ana Maria's shoulder. "Can't you make an exception for her?" he asked.

Surprise cut through Ana Maria's despair. James was defending her.

"I'm sorry," the official said. "Now, if you'll excuse me, I must tend to these folks." Behind Ana Maria were a man and woman dressed as cowboys.

Ana Maria backed up and leaned against the wall. How could she have been so stupid? She had only looked at the advertisement once, her eyes focused on the prize money. Now, she had wasted Mrs. Wagner's time and deceived Papá. All for nothing. Tomorrow, her vihuela would be gone, and with it, her dreams.

The hallway began to fill up with performers and spectators. Mrs. Wagner draped an arm around Ana Maria's shoulders. "I'm sorry, honey."

"It wouldn't have killed that fellow to let her perform," James said.

Ana Maria heard the pity in his voice and stared at her shoes. If she saw pity in James's eyes, she would cry.

"I don't think we should leave until you play your song, Ana Maria," James said.

"You're not helping, James," Mrs. Wagner said. "Come on. I'll treat us all to an ice cream cone." She gently turned Ana Maria in the direction of the front door.

Before they had taken three steps, a barrage of angry Spanish echoed down the hall. Ana Maria looked up. Papá was striding toward her, his face red and his eyes ablaze.

"¿Qué haces aquí?" he barked.

Ana Maria stood frozen. She could not explain why she had lied to him here in the hall with James and his mother and dozens of strangers listening.

"Hello, Mr. Garcia," Mrs. Wagner said. "It's wonderful that you could make it after all, but sadly, there's been a mix-up. Ana Maria won't be able to perform tonight. You have a very disappointed little girl."

Papá shot Mrs. Wagner a puzzled look. Then he shifted his stare back to Ana Maria. "Javier and Juana stopped by the Torrez house on their way home from Bayard to see how the roofing was going. They had no idea you were sleeping at their house tonight."

Ana Maria's stomach plunged.

"So, I went to their house to check on you. But you weren't there. Imagine how I felt when Gabriela told me where you were. When I found out you had *lied* to me."

Shame flushed Ana Maria's face.

"And for what?" Papá thrust out an arm, pointing to where five Anglo girls carrying batons and dressed in majorette uniforms walked by. "To prance around onstage? That's not the proper place for a girl. Haven't I raised you better?" He held out his hand. "Give me the vihuela."

Ana Maria stepped back.

"Dámelo!" Papá's voice was hard.

This was her last chance, her only chance, to play Mamá's corrido.

"Un momentito, Papá." Ana Maria's voice was quiet but firm.

She took the vihuela out of its case, squared her back against the wall, and placed her fingers on the opening chords. Since she could not bear to look at Papá's angry face, she looked at James instead. He smiled and nodded. Her old friend understood what she was about to do.

A line had formed in front of the table. The official was checking off performers, and a woman was taking tickets from spectators. Ana Maria swallowed. She had wanted an audience. Now she had one.

As she strummed the opening chord, everyone turned to stare. The official frowned. He put down his clipboard and headed toward her. James stepped in front of him.

Ana Maria drew in a deep breath and opened her heart to all the love and longing she felt for Mamá. Then, she began to sing. The words rippled in waves across the growing crowd. Her fingers flew across the strings, every note ringing true. She felt Mamá's presence around her, beside her, within her.

Everyone in the hall had stopped walking and talking. All eyes were fixed on her. The official wore a look of wonder, and Mrs. Wagner had one hand pressed to her heart. James's smile was proud.

"Los hombres debilitados teñidos de negro por la tierra," Ana Maria sang. She shifted her gaze to Papá. "Sosteniendo el zinc azul plateada."

All anger had vanished from Papá's face. Now, his eyes brimmed with tears.

Ana Maria reached the final verses. The corrido had started as a ballad to Mamá, but events transformed it. Now, it was a song about love and loss and forgiveness. It was a song for Papá too.

Giró su rostro hacia la pared.
Es mi culpa que aquí estés.
No, mi amor, ella le dijo.
Escaparemos juntos, no debes temer.

Entonces los mineros y las esposas de los mineros
Al unísono con sus manos unidas bloquearán.
Su propósito común rompió la maldición;
Siendo la unidad su talismán.

Se levantaron de las profundidades subterráneas,
Sus voces se levantaron en el poder.
De frente en pie ante la bestia
Las familias mineras sin cobardía en su haber.

Cucuy regresó a su guarida.
Las familias vitorearon en gloria.
Sus sueños les pertenecían una vez más;
Ahora han escuchado su historia.

Pero presten atención a esta advertencia,
todos quienes escuchan:
El acobardado Cucuy no se ha ido.
Si perdemos nuestra solidaridad,
En una canción futura habrá venido.

Ana Maria's voice hung on the last note for several seconds before fading. She tingled, and her body and the vihuela felt as one. She had done her best to follow her dream like Mamá had wanted. For this brief moment, she had been a corridista.

There was a split second of silence before James whooped and began to clap. Everyone else joined in.

The official came up to Ana Maria and clasped her hand. "I must say, Miss. That was spectacular. We'll have another talent show next summer. Please, I beg you, audition for it." He squeezed her hand. "I guarantee you'll be on that stage."

As people entered the auditorium, many of them complimented Ana Maria and asked if she was performing. After the auditorium doors shut, Mrs. Wagner told Ana Maria, "We'll wait outside for you. Come on, James."

"Just a second." James turned to Ana Maria. "That was really beautiful."

A warm glow filled her. "Thanks."

"I heard the word *Cucuy*. I know that's a monster from Mexican folktales, but what was the rest of the song about?"

Ana Maria quickly summarized her corrido.

James' brows furrowed. "So when Cucuy hurts your mom and steals her dreams, was that supposed to be my dad?"

Ana Maria winced. "No! I'm really sorry, James. I never should have said that your dad killed my mom. It isn't true, and I didn't mean it."

"Okay, I'm glad you didn't mean it, but then who is Cucuy?"

"Cucuy is lots of things. It's the mine where men die. It's the ax that cut my mom's foot. It's not having enough money to pay the doctor." Ana Maria glanced at Papá, who stood on the other side of the hall, watching her. "Cucuy is also people who don't believe a girl can be a corridista. Cucuy is complicated."

James nodded. "But Cucuy is the Empire Zinc Company, too, right? Because if the company had put plumbing and a gas stove in your house, your mom wouldn't have cut her foot while chopping wood."

Ana Maria smiled. This was what she had been trying to tell him on the day their friendship ended. He finally understood. "Yes, Cucuy is also Empire Zinc."

"Okay, I get it." James shoved his hands into his pockets. "You know, your mom was a really nice lady, and I'm really sorry she died."

Ana Maria's eyes prickled. "Thanks, James."

He headed down the hall.

Ana Maria caressed the neck of the vihuela, feeling its familiar smoothness for the final time. Then she put the instrument back in the case, walked over to Papá, and handed the case to him. "It's tuned and polished."

Papá gently pushed the case back toward her. "Even if we have to sleep under the stars," he said in a voice thick with emotion, "I will never sell your vihuela." He pulled Ana Maria into a hug. "Mija, you are a corridista."

Chapter 13

August 1 came and went. Papá did not pay the rent. With the vihuela off-limits, they had nothing left to sell. A few days later, desperate for a break from the tension and hungry for meat to feed their families, Papá and Javier Talamante went into the desert to hunt mule deer.

Ana Maria was shaking out a rug on the front step when she saw someone walking down the road. She squinted, wondering if it was a trick of the light. In all the years she had known James Wagner, she had never seen him on the Mexican American side of town.

James waved and turned into the yard. He wore an uncertain smile, as if he was not sure he was welcome. "Hi, Ana Maria."

"Hi, James." They had not seen each other since the night of the talent show.

He looked around the yard. "So, what are you doing today?" He spoke casually, as if he had not spent most of the last year giving her the cold shoulder.

"Chores." She shook the rug. "Then I'm going to Bayard with Linda Bradley."

James nodded. "I thought you might want to go swimming. My mom said she would drive me and a friend to the Silver City pool."

Me and a friend. The phrase tugged a load of memories behind it. Them splashing in a kiddie pool in the Wagners' yard when they were toddlers. Playing board games in a fort they'd constructed under the dining room table. Racing bicycles around the neighborhood.

Ana Maria had missed James. But their friendship had always been kept on the Anglo side of town, in James's house, and in his world. He did not understand Ana Maria's world at all.

"I'm not allowed to swim in the Silver City pool," she said.

He drew back. "What? That's not true."

Ana Maria sighed. "Yeah, it is. There is a sign right on the entrance gate. 'No dogs or Mexicans allowed.'"

James clicked his tongue in disgust. "Sheesh. I didn't know that."

"Why don't you ask Larry to go with you?"

"He's in Texas visiting his grandma."

"Maybe Peter wants to go swimming." Ana Maria did not try to keep the contempt out of her voice.

James made a face. "Peter is kind of a jerk."

"I could have told you that a long time ago."

"As you know, it takes me a while to figure things out." James kicked a pebble. "Instead of the pool, then, maybe we could go wading in the creek?"

Ana Maria was confused. Was James here because he was bored with Larry out of town, or was he here because he wanted to be friends again? "I have to be at the Bradleys' in a half hour," she said.

"Oh yeah." James's face fell. "Why are you going to Bayard anyway?"

"We're going to the union hall. Linda and I are sending out letters requesting donations from other unions."

"Donations for what?"

From inside the house, Ana Maria heard the angry whistle of the kettle. "My water is boiling. Come inside, James."

In the kitchen, Ana Maria used a hot pad to lift the kettle off the wood stove. She poured some boiling water into the tub of dishes in the sink and dumped the rest into a second tub for rinsing.

"So you have to start a fire to heat your water?"

Ana Maria looked over her shoulder. James stood in the kitchen doorway, looking around the room like it was a museum of some foreign culture.

"Yep." She grabbed a pitcher off the shelf and filled it from the water barrel. Then she added this cold water to the dish tubs. "Anyway, the donations are for us. The mine families." She began scrubbing eggs off Papá's breakfast plate.

"What do you need donations for?"

Ana Maria looked at James in disbelief. "The strike has lasted for nine months. We need money for food and gas and rent and everything." She dipped the plate in the rinse tub and then set it on the drain board.

James grabbed the towel hanging on a hook on the wall. He picked up the plate from the drain board and began to dry it. "Can I come with you?"

"Where?"

"To the union hall."

Ana Maria stopped washing again and looked at him. "Really?"

"Yeah. I can stuff envelopes."

"You'd be helping the union. What would your dad think?"

"Well—I know, but—if you guys don't have enough food, and you don't have hot water . . ." He looked out the kitchen door into the living room. "I bet my dad doesn't realize things are this bad."

Ana Maria saw her house through James's eyes. The tired sofa, the scratched table, the worn rug on the floor, the small living space. So different from the Wagners' house.

"Okay," she said. "You can come with me."

A few eyebrows rose when James, the son of a mine supervisor, walked into the union hall. But when Ana Maria said he was there to help, no one objected. James did stuff envelopes with Ana Maria, Linda, and Mrs. Bradley, but not many. He was too busy taking in the action around him.

The hall was buzzing with activity. At one table, a couple of women were typing letters. Another woman cranked out copies of the letters on a mimeograph machine. The grocery distribution committee was meeting in one corner of the room, while in the opposite corner Scott Bradley was leading the political action committee.

At one point, James whispered to Ana Maria, "These people don't look like communists."

Mrs. Bradley leaned across the table. "What does a communist look like?"

James's face turned beet red. "Uh, I don't . . . sorry."

Mrs. Bradley laughed. "I'm teasing. I bet you've got some questions about what we're doing here. Would you like someone to give you a tour?"

James looked at Ana Maria. She nodded. "Yeah, sure," James said.

The political action committee was just ending, so Mrs. Bradley called her husband over and introduced him to James.

"You're Rick Wagner's son, aren't you?" Mr. Bradley asked.

"Yes, sir," James said.

Mr. Bradley smiled. "Come on. I'll show you around, and your father is welcome, too, if he ever wants to visit."

Ana Maria watched Mr. Bradley explain the signs on the walls and introduce James to the other adults in the hall. When James returned to the table thirty minutes later, he looked more relaxed. "I think I get it now."

"Get what?" Ana Maria asked.

James spread his arms wide, indicating the hall and everyone in it. "The strike. The union. What your corrido meant. I wish my dad would come here so he could understand his workers better. But he couldn't fix things, even if he wanted to. He's a supervisor, but he doesn't own the mine."

Just then, the door to the hall flew open with a bang. José Luis Torrez barged in. He was the son of the union president. "Is Martín Garcia here?" he shouted.

An alarm bell went off in Ana Maria's head. "He's deer hunting," she said.

"I need to find him." José Luis's voice held a note of panic. "The company has an eviction order. The sheriff is at Garcia's house now."

Ana Maria stood up. "I need to go home."

Mrs. Bradley was already on her feet. "Those sneaks wait until no one is home to do their dirty work." She looked at the people around the hall. "Are we going to let Empire Zinc put Martín and Ana Maria out on the street?"

"No way!" James shouted, pumping his fist in the air.

"You heard him, folks," Mr. Bradley called. "Everyone head to the Garcia house. And spread the word on your way!"

Chapter 14

Mrs. Bradley drove back to Alba in record time, but it was not fast enough for Ana Maria. The word *eviction* pounded in her head like a hammer. This was why Papá had wanted to sell the vihuela. This was the reality he had wanted her to face. Instead, she had whined about wanting to be a corridista. *Estúpido!*

As Mrs. Bradley pulled over in front of the house, Ana Maria saw two deputies hauling a table out the front door. Four more deputies stood in the front yard, talking to Sheriff Coleman. Gabriela and her brothers and several other little boys from the neighborhood were watching over the fence. Señora Morano and some other elderly women stood along the fence too.

Ana Maria hopped out of the car and ran to Gabriela. James followed. When she looked into the yard, Ana Maria gasped. The sofa was on its side. Its cushions had fallen in the dirt. Lamps, books, pots, and pans were scattered everywhere. The painting of Benito Juárez lay against a flowerpot. A long rip cut the revolutionary's face in two.

Then a deputy emerged from the house carrying her vihuela case.

"No!" Ana Maria cried. She tried to push past the old women to reach the gate. Mrs. Bradley yanked her back.

"You'll just get in trouble," she said. "There aren't enough of us here yet. We have to wait for the miners before we take any action."

"What if they don't arrive in time?" Ana Maria knew what happened during evictions. After the renter's possessions were removed from the house, the sheriff changed the locks. If that happened, she and Papá would be homeless.

Then inspiration struck.

"We just have to slow the deputies down," she whispered. "I have an idea." She pulled James and Gabriela into a huddle and laid out her plan. Gabriela passed on the orders to her brothers and their friends. The boys grinned with delight and scampered around the fence to the other side of the house.

A minute later, a clump of dirt rocketed over the fence. It struck a deputy exiting the house with an armful of blankets, knocking off his cowboy hat. A thrill shot through Ana Maria when she realized the man was Carrot-head.

"What the heck!" Carrot-head dropped the blankets as more dirt clods rained down on him and the other deputies. The men bolted through the gate to chase the giggling gang. But this neighborhood was the boys' playground, and they knew every hiding place.

"Never mind them!" Sheriff Coleman yelled. He walked into the road. "Come back so we can get this job done."

"Now's our chance!" James said. He darted through the gate with Ana Maria and Gabriela on his heels. He picked up a lamp and a couch cushion and ran around the house to enter through the back porch. Gabriela picked up the pile of blankets and followed him. Ana Maria grabbed her vihuela. Once inside the house, she tucked the vihuela into the back of the hallway closet, which the deputies had already emptied.

When she returned to the yard, the deputies were straggling back from their failed pursuit of the boys. Sheriff Coleman was yelling at them. As Ana Maria bent down to pick up a stack of framed photographs of Mamá, the gate creaked. She looked up to see Linda Bradley slip into the yard and run to where James and Gabriela were trying to lift the table. Ana Maria went to help. The four of them carried the table into the house through the back door.

Just as they set the table down in the living room, Ana Maria heard people enter through the front door. She motioned to the others to stand flat against the living room wall where they could not be seen from the hallway.

"Grab that table," commanded a voice Ana Maria recognized as Carrot-head's.

"But didn't we already—" one of the deputies began.

"Move it!"

The deputies grunted as they lifted the table and carried it out the front door. As they left, a line of old women carrying dresser drawers entered through the back door. Señora Morano led the way. She grinned at Ana Maria and whispered, "We'll return these items and go back out-side for more."

Back in the yard, Sheriff Coleman was talking to Seño-ra Diaz, an eighty-four-year-old with a face like a crumpled bag. She was holding Mamá's teapot.

"Now see here," the sheriff said. "You put that down right now."

"No hablo inglés," Señora Diaz said.

Ana Maria bit back a smile. The old woman spoke perfect English.

"Bajo!" the sheriff shouted. "Down!"

Señora Diaz looked at him like he had suddenly sprout-ed three heads.

Meanwhile, Gabriela's brothers and their playmates had snuck into the yard and were returning items to the house faster than the deputies could carry them out. Carrot-head kept trying to grab the Talamante brothers, but they were too quick.

Ana Maria and her friends took advantage of the con-fusion. They raced through the back door with anything they could carry.

She and James were carrying the rocking chair across the yard when Sheriff Coleman snapped. "If you all don't get out of this yard, you're under arrest!"

The deputies grabbed their handcuffs. Carrot-head took a step toward Ana Maria.

Car horns blared in the distance. Everyone turned to look. Señor Talamante's pickup truck came around the corner, leading a convoy of six cars. A dozen men rode in the truck bed. The vehicles parked and men tumbled out of the cars. Some were Anglo and some were Mexican American. All were miners. The men, including Papá, stood shoulder to shoulder in front of the fence.

It was a standoff. The old women and children stood in a cluster on one side of the yard. Thirty miners faced them outside the gate. Trapped in between were Sheriff Coleman and six deputies.

"Are you going to fill your jail with old women and children again, Sheriff?" Papá asked.

"Now see here, Garcia," the sheriff said. "I've got to carry out this eviction order."

Papá narrowed his eyes. "You're going to put a man and his eleven-year-old daughter out on the street for an overdue rent of thirty-eight bucks? I thought you were better than that."

The air grew thick with tension. Sheriff Coleman eyed the crowd of miners, as if uncertain of what to do. Suddenly, another car raced around the corner. It squealed to a stop in front of the gate, and Scott Bradley leaped out.

"Hold up, Sheriff!" Mr. Bradley waved a piece of paper as if it were a shield. "Judge Sanders issued a stay of that eviction order. Garcia has ten days to pay his rent."

The sheriff grabbed the paper and quickly scanned it. A wave of relief washed over his face. "Okay, boys. This order is valid. Let's head out."

As the deputies and the sheriff drove away, Papá walked to Ana Maria and put an arm around her shoulder. "My brave hija," he said quietly.

Then he faced the crowd. "Thank you, my friends, for coming to our rescue. If not for you, Ana Maria and I would not have a roof over our heads tonight."

Papá paused and swallowed several times. He looked at the ground and took several shaking breaths. Ana Maria felt her heart twinge.

"This year has been hard," Papá said finally. "After Teresa died, the hospital bills took everything we had. I'm afraid that unless the strike ends tomorrow, I won't be able to pay Empire Zinc even after ten days."

Ana Maria did not hesitate. "Yes, we can, Papá. We'll sell my vihuela."

Behind her, James gasped.

Papá shook his head vigorously. "No, mija. I promised you. Never."

Señor Talamante stepped forward. He dug his wallet out of his back pocket and removed some bills from it. "An injury to one is an injury to all," he said. Then he took off his hat and dropped the money inside. "I'm starting this collection to help my union brother Martín raise rent money. Times are tough for all of us right now, but please give what you can."

The hat was passed from man to man. Some put bills in the hat. Others dropped in a few coins. When Señora

Morano pressed five dollars into Papá's hand, his chin began to tremble.

Ana Maria knew Papá would be humiliated if he broke down in front of his friends and neighbors. He needed time to collect himself. She ran into the house and retrieved her vihuela case from the closet.

When she returned to the yard, Señor Talamante was handing Papá the hat full of money, and Papá was struggling to hold his emotions in check.

"Thank you, everyone, for your generosity," Ana Maria said, drawing attention away from Papá. "How about some music to celebrate?" She strummed the vihuela and began to sing.

The celebration lasted a long time. The miners carried the rest of the possessions into the house, where Señora Morano supervised everything being restored to order. Women returning from the picket line came over with food and drink.

When Ana Maria grew tired, she handed the vihuela off to a miner who could play. Then she ran around with Gabriela, James, Linda, and the little boys until the sky grew dusky.

After everyone had gone home, Ana Maria lay on one side of the couch, with Papá on the other side. Her feet were propped up against his legs.

"Did we get enough money to pay the rent?" she asked through a jaw-splitting yawn.

"Thirty-six dollars and forty-seven cents," Papá said. "I can manage the last little bit." His smile was tired but grateful. "Our neighbors are good people."

"Sí." Ana Maria's eyelids were heavy.

He nudged her foot with his leg. "How about tomorrow we visit Mamá's grave? You can play your corrido for her."

Ana Maria fell asleep with a smile on her face.

Epilogue

SUMMER 1952

*A*na Maria squirted some dish soap into the sink and cranked on the hot-water faucet. As she scrubbed the dishes, she thought about the long, hard fight it had taken to get this indoor plumbing.

The strike had lasted until January 1952, when Empire Zinc finally agreed to negotiate. On January 24, Union Local 890 approved a contract that gave workers a forty-cent raise, vacation benefits, and pay for every minute the miners spent underground. Best of all, in Ana Maria's opinion, Empire Zinc agreed to pipe water to all company-owned property on the Mexican American side of town.

The miners and their families had remained united, and Empire Zinc had listened to their collective voices.

"Hurry up, mija!" Papá called. "Or you'll be late for jail."

Ana Maria grinned and quickly finished the dishes. An hour later, she was behind bars for the second time in her life. But this time, she was not afraid. The cell was just a movie set. When the director called, "Cut!" Ana Maria was free to leave.

Shortly after the strike ended, Michael Wilson had returned to Alba with a team of directors and producers. Now they were in town making a movie called *Salt of the Earth*. Mr. Wilson had created a fake town with fake families and a fake company, but the facts followed the Empire Zinc Mine strike closely. The mine company was the villain, and the miners and their families were the heroes.

One of those heroes was standing next to Ana Maria. It was the same woman she had stood next to one year earlier when she had been locked in jail. Once again, the woman started to bang her tin cup against the bars.

"Cut!" the director shouted. "We aren't ready for the cup banging yet."

"Oh, sorry," said the woman. "I got angry, just like I did the day they arrested us."

The director smiled. "Well, it's good that you've got the real emotion to fuel your acting. That's why we hired local people to play these parts instead of professional actors. Now, let's take it from the top."

Soon, Ana Maria was chanting along with the women and children packed into the cell. "Queremos comida. Queremos bebidas. Queremos baños."

She had to work to keep from smiling. Unlike for the woman beside her, this scene did not stir up old feelings of anger. Although she was behind bars, Ana Maria felt freer than she had in a long time.

Mr. Wilson had told Ana Maria that *Salt of the Earth* had a happy ending. She had found her own happy ending too. She and James were friends again. He stopped by her house a few times a week, often bringing Larry. They usually went to Gabriela's house, and then the four of them would go to the creek or play tag or just talk.

Ana Maria's happy ending did not include Mamá, of course. The ache of that loss would never leave her. But she and Papá now visited Mamá's grave every Sunday.

Up there on the hillside, Papá told Ana Maria stories she had never heard. Stories from Mamá's childhood. Stories about how Papá had fallen in love with Mamá. Stories about Ana Maria's birth. On those Sunday afternoons, it was almost like their family was whole again. Ana Maria brought her vihuela along. She sang for Mamá, and Papá always asked her to play "The Miners' Lament" for him.

The chant filled the small cell. "Queremos . . . queremos . . ." *We want . . . we want . . .*

The beat pulsed in Ana Maria's temples as if the words were part of her blood. Maybe they were. Perhaps that was the happiest part of her happy ending. Ana Maria had found her voice. Through her corrido, she had managed to peel back the veil over Papá's heart so he could understand what she felt in her own.

When *Salt of the Earth* was released in theaters, Ana Maria planned to go see it. Then she would decide. Which interpretation did a better job of giving voice to the voiceless—*Salt of the Earth* or "The Miners' Lament"?

Author's Note

This is a work of fiction, and Ana Maria is a character of my imagination. However, the Empire Zinc Mine strike really did occur, and an independent movie production company did make a movie about it called *Salt of the Earth*. Many of the challenges Ana Maria faced were based on challenges that Mexican American families faced during this event.

The historical source I relied on most was *On Strike and On Film: Mexican American Families and Blacklisted Filmmakers in Cold War America* by Ellen R. Baker. I also read articles from the *Silver City Daily Press* archives and personal accounts preserved on the Salt of the Earth Recovery Project website. You can read these firsthand accounts at saltoftheearthrecoveryproject.wordpress.com.

There are many books about Mexican corridos. I used *Mexican-American Folklore* by John O. West, *The Mexican Corrido: A Feminist Analysis* by María Herrera-Sobek, and *Corridos in Migrant Memory* by Martha I. Chew Sánchez. While many corridos tell a straightforward history of an event, I chose to have Ana Maria's lyrics tell a more fantastical story as a metaphor for what she was experiencing in her life.

The town of Alba is fictional, but it's loosely based on the town of Hanover, New Mexico, where the Empire Zinc Mine was based. I changed the names of all participants in the strike and subsequent making of the movie, except one person—screenwriter Michael Wilson. He worked with Independent Productions Corporation, a movie company formed by some directors and producers who had been blacklisted by Hollywood because they were suspected of being communists. Wilson did come to the picket line to observe the strike in action.

The events on the picket line closely follow the historical chronology of the Empire Zinc Mine strike. The actions of the sheriff, deputies, judges, and union leaders that are featured in the story are drawn from historical sources. The strike began on October 17, 1950. After striking miners were prohibited from blocking the mine road, Union Local 890 did vote to allow female relatives of the miners to take over the picket line. There were tensions between husbands and wives in some families over whether or not women should march on the picket line and what responsibilities the men should take around the house.

The violence depicted in the story is historically accurate. Female picketers threw rocks at cars, pushed cars down the road, and used red pepper and pins against deputies. The sheriff did order tear gas thrown at the women, and in two instances, deputies struck picketers with their cars, hitting a fourteen-year-old girl and a seventy-five-year-old woman. Also, on June 15, 1951, the sheriff arrested and jailed fifty-three women and an unspecified number of children. Other male and female leaders were arrested and jailed periodically during the strike.

The strike ended when Empire Zinc finally agreed to negotiate in early January 1952, and on January 24, members voted to approve the new contract. That final contract included a promise from Empire Zinc to add indoor plumbing to all its company properties, including those on the Mexican American side of town.

The movie *Salt of the Earth* was released in 1954 and is still available online. The final cast featured nine locals who were members of Local 890 or wives of members. A production committee included members of the film company, Local 890, and the Ladies Auxiliary. This committee organized the logistics of building sets and props and feeding and transporting actors. The locals on the committee also were responsible for making sure the movie ran true to life. If a scene was not accurate in its details, the locals challenged the filmmakers to reshoot it. While the final movie did not please everyone, filmmakers collaborated with the miners and their families in an effort to portray events correctly.

Photos

A mural on the side of the union hall in Bayard, New Mexico, shows the striking women.

Actors in Salt of the Earth carry picket signs, including one that says, "We want sanitation not discrimination."

El Lamento de los Mineros

Amigos, vengan a escuchar mi historia de aflicción.
Ante ustedes he sido enviado
Para compartir esta historia sobre personas sencillas.
Aquí está su lamento.

Siendo el diez de octubre,
Frescura caía al anochecer,
Cuando la mujer llamada Teresa
Olía el almizcle corromper.

Mientras cortaba leña
Ella la noche observó.
Y unos ojos rojos brillantes, mandíbulas dentadas—
Ella lo reconoció.

Cucuy lanzó un llamado
Con apetito indómito,
Hambriento por la hija de Teresa
Quién fuera permanecía durmiendo.

Teresa de pie se puso para defender
Al bebé que dentro de la casa permanecía.
Cucuy llegó a un acuerdo con ella—
Donde a cambio de un préstamo la vida de la niña le daría.

La mujer la dio siguiendo su voluntad;
Ella no tenía otra opción.
Por la vida de su hija se debía sacrificar
Ofreció la voz profunda de su corazón.

Aún cuando Teresa pudiera hablar,
Tenía prohibido revelar
Todos los pensamientos que habian dentro de su corazón
Que ocultos para siempre deberían estar.

Por supuesto su espíritu se desgarraría
Teresa tuvo que quebrar su maldición.
Así volvió hacia su amada
Pero algo peor encontró.

Mi amor, rogó, *por favor escucha.*
Cucuy ha silenciado mis sueños.
Pero cuando la miró a los ojos
Teresa solo pudo gritar.

Dentro del hombre que Teresa amaba
Moraba la bestia de ojos rojos.
Enfrentó al minero contra la esposa del minero;
Para hacer en su disputa festejos.

Entonces Teresa se unió a otras mujeres
Cuyo sueño también fue atrapado.
Marcharon. Bailaron. Se enfrentaron.
Pero todo fue infundado.

El monstruo arrasó contra ellos,
Con sus garras y afilados colmillos.
Los capturó en su calabozo
Y los encerró entre cadenas.

Teresa examinó la oscura celda
Para su sorpresa sus ojos vieran
Atrapados bajo tierra y sin voz
Hombres con ojos de mineros eran.

Los hombres debilitados teñidos de negro por la tierra
Sosteniendo el zinc azul plateada.
Su amada la miró enmudecida
Pues su alma también había sido silenciada.

Giró su rostro hacia la pared.
Es mi culpa que aquí estés.
No, mi amor, ella le dijo.
Escaparemos juntos, no debes temer.

Entonces los mineros y las esposas de los mineros
Al unísono con sus manos unidas bloquearán.
Su propósito común rompió la maldición;
Siendo la unidad su talismán.

Se levantaron de las profundidades subterráneas,
Sus voces se levantaron en el poder.
De frente en pie ante la bestia
Las familias mineras sin cobardía en su haber.

Cucuy regresó a su guarida.
Las familias vitorearon en gloria.
Sus sueños les pertenecían una vez más;
Ahora han escuchado su historia.

Pero presten atención a esta advertencia, todos quienes escuchan:
El acobardado Cucuy no se ha ido.
Si perdemos nuestra solidaridad,
En una canción futura habrá venido.

The Miners' Lament

Friends, come hear my tale of woe.
To you I have been sent
To share the story of a simple people.
This is their lament.

It was the tenth of October,
A crisp fall at dusk,
When the woman named Teresa
Smelled the rank musk.

As she chopped firewood
She looked into the night.
Bright red eyes and jagged jaws—
She recognized the sight.

Cucuy had come a-calling
With a savage appetite,
Hungry for Teresa's child
Who was sleeping out of sight.

Teresa stood to defend
The babe inside the home.
Cucuy struck a deal with her—
For the child's life, a loan.

The woman gave it willingly;
She had no other choice.
For her daughter's life she sacrificed
Her heart's deepest voice.

While Teresa could still speak,
She was forbidden to reveal
The thoughts that lay inside her heart,
Which must forever stay concealed.

Sure it would crush her spirit
Teresa had to break the curse.
So she turned to her beloved
But there found something worse.

My love, she begged, *please listen.*
Cucuy has silenced my dreams.
But when he looked into her eyes
Teresa could only scream.

Inside the man Teresa loved
Dwelled the red-eyed beast.
It pitted miner against miner's wife;
On their disputes it made a feast.

So Teresa joined other women
whose dreams had, too, been caught.
They marched. They danced. They took a stand.
But it was all for naught.

The monster plowed straight into them,
Claws out and sharpened fangs.
It hauled them to its dungeon lair
And locked them up in chains.

Teresa surveyed the darkened cell
And saw to her surprise
Trapped underground and voiceless
Were men with miners' eyes.

The weakened men were black with dirt
And held zinc so silver-blue.
Her beloved stared mutely back at her;
His soul had been silenced too.

He turned his face to the wall.
It's my fault that you are here.
No, my love, she said to him.
We'll escape together, never fear.

So, the miners and the miners' wives
Locked hands in unison.
Their common purpose broke the curse;
Unity, their talisman.

They rose up from deep underground,
Their voices raised in power.
Standing tall before the beast
The mine families didn't cower.

Cucuy slunk back to its lair.
The families cheered in glory.
Their dreams belonged to them once more;
Now you have heard their story.

But heed this caution, listeners all:
Cucuy is cowed, not gone.
If we lose our solidarity,
It'll return in future song.

Timeline

Oct. 17, 1950 — Strike begins.

March 1951
Empire Zinc Company launches a back-to-work campaign, flooding workers' mailboxes with letters encouraging them to end the strike.

June 7, 1951
Empire Zinc announces it will reopen the mine, and the Grant County sheriff deputizes several local men to help him keep the peace on the picket line.

June 11, 1951
Strikers and strikebreakers face off at the picket line. The sheriff arrests eleven men, but other miners take their places on the line, and the picket line holds.

June 12, 1951
Grant County judge A. W. Marshall issues a temporary injunction preventing the strikers from blocking the road to the mine entrance. That evening, Local 890 votes to permit female relatives of the strikers to take their places on the picket line.

June 13, 1951
The women take over the picket line.

June 29, 1951
Judge Marshall rules that the injunction against the strikers also applies to the women and children on the picket line.

July 9, 1951
Judge Marshall rules the injunction blocking the picket line is permanent.

July 11, 1951
The permanent injunction goes into effect. Three hundred women show up to defy the injunction.

July 12, 1951
Deputy Marvin Mosely drives his car into fourteen-year-old picketer Rachel Juárez.

July 23, 1951
Judge Marshall rules that Mine-Mill International, Local 890, and six local union leaders are in contempt of court for violating the injunction.

Aug. 23, 1951
Five cars carrying strikebreakers drive through the picket line as women try to hold them back. Four picketers are seriously injured.

Jan. 1952 — Empire Zinc agrees to negotiate with the union.

Jan. 24, 1952
Striking workers unanimously vote to approve a new contract with Empire Zinc. The contract grants them higher pay and better benefits.

Mar. 10, 1952
Judge Marshall fines the union $37,750 for violating the injunction.

Sept. 1952
Six union leaders receive 90-day jail sentences for their violation of the injunction.

About the Author

Judy Dodge Cummings is a former history teacher and the author of over twenty-five fiction and nonfiction books for children. She lives in south-central Wisconsin. Her other book in the I Am America series is *When the Earth Dragon Trembled: A Story of Chinatown During the San Francisco Earthquake and Fire*.

About the Consultant

Zakery R. Muñoz was born and raised in Albuquerque, New Mexico. He received his MA in Rhetoric and Writing at the University of New Mexico with a specific focus on rhetorical history and the rhetoric of citizenship. He was a Project Coordinator for the Salt of the Earth Recovery Project that was featured in an NPR piece titled "And They Will Inherit It." His work has afforded him fellowships including the Graduate University Fellowship at Syracuse University to complete his PhD in Composition and Cultural Rhetoric.

About the Illustrator

Eric Freeberg has illustrated over twenty-five books for children, and has created work for magazines and ad campaigns. He was a winner of the 2010 London Book Fair's Children's Illustration Competition; the 2010 Holbein Prize for Fantasy Art, International Illustration Competition, Japan Illustrators' Association; Runner-Up, 2013 SCBWI Magazine Merit Award; Honorable Mention, 2009 SCBWI Don Freeman Portfolio Competition; and 2nd Prize, 2009 Clymer Museum's Annual Illustration Invitational. He was also a winner of the Elizabeth Greenshields Foundation Award.

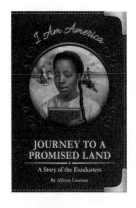